For new and upcoming releases visit

www.kimharryauthor.com

The Past Should Stay Dead

ISBN: 978-1-7397432-0-8

Published by Pegbag Publishing.

First Printing, 2022

Dedication

To all *my* estate friends.

Thanks for always supporting me

xxx

Beechwood Estate Series

Book 2

THE PAST SHOULD STAY DEAD

Kim Harry

PROLOGUE

1996

From that moment on, the world seemed silent. Blood seeped from the boy's lifeless body and stillness consumed theirs.

Against a blue summers sky and high on steel scaffolding, the star-crossed teenage lovers Heather and Jamie had watched their friend and ally fall into the freshly dug builder's trench below. He still had the blue plastic bag full of drugs that he had risked his life searching for, clasped in his hand.

The only sound to break the silence inside their confused heads was the constant screaming coming from the far side of the building site. Dexter, Heather's pain in the arse ex-boyfriend, had been blackmailing the girls, so their friend had reciprocated by instigating a revenge beating.

After a few white lies in the ears of the homophobic Thompson brothers, Dexter was now being beaten within an inch of his life for being bent. They had stripped him bare and were still kicking him as he lay in a puddle of his own piss and blood. Even though his screams and whimpering sighs were horrendous, they were nothing compared to the sound of the boy's skull hitting that shiny metal digger and falling to his fate in the rubble below.

Heather tried to pull her girlfriend away from her stance. With eyes wide shut, Jamie had fixated her glance on her only true friend. And he had bestowed his final glance in life on her.

The Welsh breeze whipped through the surrounding Caerphilly mountains. It carried the distant squawking of police sirens, forcing reality back to its rightful owners. They had to get moving.

With a white-knuckle shaky grip, the girls climbed down from the scaffolding. As they sneaked past the commotion hand in hand, weaving in and out of the poles and over the hard rubble, Wayne Thompson clocked them.

'Oi Lezzas, where do you think you're going?' He signalled to his brother Kevin to stop them, so the younger of the two ran out in front of them, smiling at them with the gap from his missing tooth. Jamie had knocked it out in a previous battle where Wayne had intended to rape her. If her friend hadn't come to her rescue that time, he would have succeeded. Wayne gave the girls a threatening once over with his judgemental eyes.

'Heather, I'm surprised at you, so you're the bitch that Jamie has been shagging. You're disgusting, the both of you.' He picked up Dexter by the hair to watch the girls, but he was already out of it. He couldn't control his legs to stand, so was just leaning into Wayne to keep his balance.

'No wonder you gave her the elbow Dexter, looks like Webster was playing games with us when he told us you were a faggot. Sorry, Matey for all this. No hard feelings though, yeah.' He dropped Dexter to the floor, and he hit his head hard on the concrete before moving his insults to Jamie.

'So you're not Webster's girlfriend either, then Jamie. I knew he was covering your dykey arse. You look more like a man than he does.'

Jamie wanted to beat the crap out of Wayne, but Heather pulled her back.

'We'll have to pay the lying scum a visit after this.'

'He's dead, you bastard. We were watching you up there on the scaffold and he lost his balance. This is all your fucking fault. If it wasn't for you attacking me and trying to rape me, he wouldn't have been up there.'

'Well, well. You're not having much luck lately, are you?' His smile made Jamie feel physically sick. 'You know, this is all you and your slut of a girlfriend's fault for fannying around together. If you were normal and not a perverted lezza, then none of us would be here.'

Wayne walked towards them and spat in Jamie's face.

'It's a good job he's dead. We will make sure that this is all over the estate tomorrow, so everyone will know about you two. Your dad's gonna go ballistic, you know how much of a psycho he is. He's worse than our old man.'

Both fathers had forbidden the girls to see each other and if the true intentions of today's escapades ever got out, there would be dire consequences. They were newly in love and in a secret relationship. But the odds were continually being stacked against them. Rumours were rife, and Jamie's abusive homophobic father had already received a limp warning by Heather's God-fearing one that she should leave Heather alone. Jimmy senior would beat his family regularly for antics far less serious than his daughter's Sapphic ways. Nobody brought trouble to their door, and if they did, they faced the wrath of Jimmy Taylor, whatever their size or gender.

As the police sirens screamed closer, they split up. The girls stumbled across the loose rubble and crawled under a broken wire fence. They ran across the car park and hid behind a storage container at the neighbouring bowling alley.

From its side view, they peered through the crack in the metal and watched the police spread out in desperate search for the perpetrators. The Thompson brothers were too fast as always and had scaled the metal fence and jumped on their bikes before the police even entered the yard.

When the paramedics arrived, they continually worked on Dexter. Although they hated him right now for causing their grief in the first place, they were both relieved when he was hoisted into the back of the ambulance with his oxygen mask in place. They could clearly see that he was moving and were grateful that he was still alive after the beating he had suffered because of them.

The bullying Thompson brothers would now be long gone and safely on their way home to the lap of their mother. Their alibi for all the crimes they had ever committed on the Welsh council estate would always be there with open arms.

After their father Frankie left to shack up with another woman and their new baby, the boys were all their mother had. She knew they were little bastards, but so was their father. It was all they had ever known. She couldn't change the past and never wanted to.

The new and improved version of the Thompson family was living on the other side of the estate. Frankie Thompson's crooked ways were paying well, and they hadn't had the decency to move far. Even though they had the money to live in a much bigger place, Beechwood estate would always be his home.

Most of the residents there looked after their own. Many of the parents had grown up on the estate themselves, enjoying the community spirit that always shone through.

Street parties for national events had the estate roads closed off and lined with bunting and happy faces. Everyone would bring something out to make-shift tables and the kids would fill their paper bowls with jelly and angel delight before scoffing down pink wafers washed down with Sunny D if you were lucky. Neighbours would dance around in their shell suits while getting pissed on cans of whatever they could afford that week, and there was always a bottle of Pomagne hidden under the table in the hands of a couple of ten-year-olds.

As much as the estate still had that community spirit, there were a lot of rotten apples that had festered amongst the good, and Frankie was one of them. There was an edge of mania about him and even though he didn't give a shit about anyone but himself, he still drove around in his brand-new BMW, throwing money at his boys just to show off whenever he saw them. He showed no remorse for breaking up their unhappy home and he would carry on, regardless.

Underground crime and gangland activity gave Frankie his passport to rule over many an unsuspecting business.

Targeting small firms for protection money was easy. The man did whatever he liked and the whole family's reputation thrived on it. He had a way of silencing people, and everybody knew that retribution from him was always served cold. Most people on the estate would pretend to admire him to avoid being targeted for whatever reason Frankie had bartered with. But it was the young scally's that were in the most danger. He relished in how some of the young lads would look up to him despite the disapproval of their parents. Even Webster's older brother had been buying his drugs from him. It was the retrieval of his blue plastic bag that had sent him to his death.

Before the police discovered the boy's body, Jamie had held on to a thin glimmer of hope that he may have still been alive. She had hoped that the police would realise that the fall had been an accident and they would help him. No one, apart from the Thompson brothers, would know that they were ever there. And they wouldn't be offering any information any time soon. But the appearance of a body bag put pay to that. As they zipped him up and carried him away, the tears from both girls were freely flowing.

The industrial area just outside Newport that housed the bowling alley and building site was now crawling with police gathering information. They were desperately trying to piece together a series of events to work with. They had acted on an anonymous phone call. A boy was in serious danger after being followed from the bowling alley, but as yet, no one had come forward with any names.

As the girls sat rigid with their backs against the container, the police were getting worryingly close. Heather felt she had to break the silence and pull them away from their impending discovery. It wasn't safe for them to be found together.

'We have to get our stories straight Jamie, as soon as the Thompson brothers start shouting their mouths off, the whole of Beechwood estate will gossip about us. My father will probably already know about Dexter from his parents, so we need to be well prepared.'

Jamie was still staring blankly into space. Nothing seemed to matter now that her only friend was gone. Heather tried to offer comfort to her but was met with stone-cold rejection.

'At least the police have found him.'

Jamie broke from her trance and shook her head in disapproval.

'They've found his corpse, Heather. Holding a stash of drugs. They will judge him as just another user. Like all the druggies on the estate scabbing around for their next fix. If the police ask you about any of this, just say nothing. You saw nothing OK. And the last time you saw Dexter was the time of the argument at the bowling alley. Don't fuck this up for us Heather, just lie your arse off if you have to.'

Jamie's harshness took Heather by surprise. She watched furtively as she stamped around the back of the container, punching the side of it in anger.

'And no one needs to know that it was him that instigated Dexter's kicking, OK. Dexter deserved it. This was all that weasel's fault, anyway. If he hadn't shot his mouth off to your father about me and you, none of this would have happened.'

Jamie still felt the need to protect the boy's name in the same way that he had always protected hers. He was her saviour from her rock and her hard place. Now that he was dead, she felt as though it had jeopardised her entire existence. Who would protect her from the hands of her father and another impending beating from the Thompson brothers now?

As Jamie walked away, Heather knew that what she said was true. The original plan was that Dexter would tell her father that he had been lying about her and Jamie's relationship and, in return, he could carry on with the pretence that he had slept with her, the best-looking girl at the school. But the boy was adamant that Dexter had to pay for what had happened to Jamie. The near-rape from the Thompson brothers was something he couldn't get out of his head. Baiting them with rumours about Dexter's sexuality was easy, and everything had seemed to be working out after their arrival at the bowling alley. If only they had watched from below instead of up in the heavens, he may still have been alive.

When Heather arrived home, her father was waiting for her at the door. Instead of the hard approach she was dreading from him, he put his arms out and hugged her.

'Heather, thank God you're OK. We've been worried sick.' The hug from him felt safe and warm and as her mother ran out to join them, she knew how lucky she was to have their stability surrounding her mess of a life.

Heather's family lived just off the estate in the large private houses. Their community was nowhere near as supportive as the Beechwood estate, and she hardly knew her neighbours. The people there had always looked down on the estate and although they were sitting right next to it, they never acknowledged its existence when telling people where they lived. Her dad was a gentle-mannered accountant. Impeccably dressed in his shiny shoes and smart suit. Her mum was a semi-retired nurse that pottered about looking after the family. Heather was their blond-haired green-eyed angel and a gift from God as they always so fondly put it.

'Dexter's parents have just got off the phone—and all I could think about was my little girl. I'm so glad you're home.'

Nothing else mattered to them, as long as she was OK.

Heather had spent the rest of the weekend alone. As she made her way down for breakfast, she overheard her mother telling her father that there had been trouble on the estate last night. She had been listening in on the newsagent's gossip while getting the morning paper and couldn't wait to get back home to tell Mr Gardner all about it.

'It was at that Jamie's street, you know, the one that has been bothering our Heather, police cars everywhere apparently. They had found one of the Webster boys dead at the building site where Dexter was attacked. Apparently, his father and Jimmy Taylor had a brawl in the street and all the estate was out egging him on to attack Taylor. According to the newsagent, he's a wife-beater and had turned on Jamie and her brother as well.'

Mr Gardner was not one for gossip, but after already meeting the man and confronting him about his daughter's involvement with Heather, he had felt a little nervous that he may have made a mistake by going to their house. He wasn't one for confrontation by any means and was glad that all the drama with Heather was over.

'Apparently, the entire estate had heard them screaming. He's not a very nice man, by all accounts. I tried to be discreet while listening, but they shut up as soon as they noticed me. She has nothing more to do with that Jamie girl and I'm making sure of it.'

Heather left them to it. She wasn't in the mood to be given any ultimatums regarding Jamie. She would go to her best friend Abi's house and hide out there for a while.

Abi had been so understanding when Heather had told her about Jamie. She never judged her once and had helped with the drama of Dexter when he outed them to her father.

The journey alongside the canal had her remembering the beginnings of her and Jamie's relationship. She hoped it hadn't all been in vain, and they could eventually get together properly when they left school that year.

When Abi opened the door to her best friend, she had found her in tears. Everything had caught up with her and she was too tired to keep it all in.

As Abi put her arms around her, she could feel how limp Heather's body had become. It was as if her old friend had given up trying to prove to everyone that she was OK and had no fight left in her. This made Abi's guilt about the quick fumble she had shared with Jamie a few days earlier appear as a lump in her throat. It was a drunken mistake, and both girls had regretted it and vowed never to tell Heather.

'I don't know what to do or where to go from here, Abi. All I know is that there was a lot of trouble coming from Jamie's house last night and they are being talked about all over the estate. Her father is a monster and if he's hurt Jamie…'

Abi could see the fear in Heather's eyes and had worried about Jamie herself. She had noticed that Jamie's body had a lot of bruises on it, old and new, and she began putting two and two together. With her mind in confusion, she blurted a damning comment out without realising.

'Someone should tell the police. He needs to be arrested. Surely that huge belt-mark that she has across her chest would be evidence enough?'

As soon as the words fell from her mouth, she knew she had dropped herself and Jamie's secret rendezvous right in the lap of the one person they vowed never to tell.

Abi held her breath as the realisation of her and Jamie's deceit played out in Heather's mind.

'What scar? How—what are you saying?'

Abi tried to offer an explanation but the more she said, the worse it sounded. It was a moment of madness; they had shared a spliff and a few cans waiting for Heather to arrive. But, when she didn't turn up, as her dad had grounded her, they were left to their own devices and had regretted it ever since.

Heather felt her world had fallen apart. The two people she thought would never betray her had taken her love and thrown it back at her. It was the last kick in the teeth in a long line of disappointment.

As soon as she arrived back home, her father grabbed his keys and told her to keep her coat on.

'I have to take you down to the police station, Heather. Dexter is awake, and they need any information that you can give them.'

In the waiting room, she had decided that she wouldn't mention Ricky Webster. Although she hated Jamie for what she had done to her; she knew it would only make things worse for his family if she mentioned his involvement. She had had enough of all the lies and deceit. There were so many victims in all this.

'Sit down, Miss Gardner. This won't take long.' The detective that interviewed her seemed mild in her manner. She explained how Dexter had said that Wayne and Kevin Thompson were to blame for all of this. Can you collaborate with this story, Miss?'

'All I know is that we were at the bowling alley and Dexter was showing off in front of his friends, as usual. The Thompson brothers came in and started calling him gay and stuff. He was trying to deny it—then threw a bowling ball at them before running off into the crowds. The next thing I knew, he was being escorted out by the security guards. I don't know if the Thompson brothers followed him out or what, as that was the last time I saw him.'

'Thank you, Miss Gardner. This is more or less the same series of events that Dexter has told us. Before you go—can you remember if you saw a Ricky Webster at the bowling alley?'

This was the question she had been dreading, but to say he wasn't at the bowling alley wasn't a lie.

'No—as I said, it was very crowded there and full of kids, but I don't think so.'

'OK, Miss Gardner, if you could just wait outside, one of my officers will escort you both out.'

As she sat on the cold hard plastic chairs, she worried about her future. She was about to go to college and had chosen law as her career path. All this made her think, did she want to be representing scum like these? On the side-table was a police training leaflet, and as she flicked through the pages, the idea was becoming more appealing. Although she had felt drained by all of this, she had to admit that there was also a little excitement. Her father took notice of the leaflet and smiled.

'It's not a bad career to have, Heather, as long as you don't mind dealing with idiots like these. Maybe a little desk job at the station or traffic police, even.'

She could hear shouting and heavy activity coming through the doors, and this startled her. Wayne and Kevin were being brought in by their father, Frankie Thompson. Heather remembered the man's face from when they were younger. He was a horrible bastard, and everyone was afraid of him. He gave her a wink and sat opposite her and her father.

When the PC came to escort them out, she was thankful. There was something about that man that made her flesh crawl.

Chapter One

1998

'Look at you, my girl, WPC Gardner.'

Heather smiled back at her mother's comment as she paraded in her uniform in front of the mirror. She couldn't quite believe it herself. Her time away at college and then the police training unit had been a welcome change from all her teenage dramas.

'What time is Gareth picking you up? I can't wait to meet him. So has he finished all of his training now too?'

'Aw Mum, don't go embarrassing me now when he arrives, yes I told you we were at the same unit.'

As Gareth pulled up outside, Carol, Heather's mum, was on the door in an instant. She approved of the handsome young man that was dating her daughter and mentioned his resemblance to a young Tom Selleck.

Finally, she felt Heather regretted her 'mistakes' as her mother would call them and had put them behind her.

Heather pushed past Carol to get into the car before an interrogation could take place. As she slid into the passenger seat, Gareth was staring out of the window and waving at her.

'For Christ' sake Gareth, she's never going to shut the door if you keep waving at her.'

'All in good time, Heather, all in good time. We want her to like me, don't we?'

'Like you, yeah—but not think you're a crackpot—drive off we're going to be late.'

Gareth wound the window down and shouted out, just to annoy Heather.

'Bye Mrs Gardner. Have a lovely day.'

The police training college that they had both attended was in Cwmbran, just outside Newport. After every hard shift, the colleagues would meet at the hotel bar and get to know each other. Gareth and Heather had hit it off from the start. Heather loved his insane sense of humour, and when they went for a night out in Cardiff for their weekend off, they found out that they had a lot more in common.

They had started the Saturday night as a group of six but were now down to the two of them. Cardiff was heaving as usual, and as they entered Club X, they practically fell through the door. The bouncer was just about to throw them out when Gareth stood to be accounted for.

'Don't you realise we are police officers, young man?'

'Yeah, yeah and I'm Peter Pan Mate. I'll let you both in, but I'm keeping my eye on you, OK.'

They thanked the bouncer and danced their way to the bar. The music was too good to keep still and as soon as they reached the dance floor; the pull of the crowd dragged them on to it. It was heaving, and it wasn't long before a bunch of good-looking lads surrounded them in tight white t-shirts and denim.

The heat from the close contact was stifling, and Heather needed a breather.

She shouted over to Gareth, but he didn't hear over the music, so when she finally caught his attention she pointed to the bar and mouthed 'I'll get us a drink.'

He nodded, and she pushed her way through the mingling bodies on the dance floor.

The queue at the bar was battling against itself, with everyone pushing themselves to the front. Heather watched as a Tori Amos lookalike at the side of her who must have only been about 18 was losing her balance and spilling drinks over everyone. It had clearly pissed off the queue and the Missy Elliot wannabe next to her was desperately trying to dodge her by keeping out of the way of her waving cider and black hand. She was just about to confront her when a slight push from the customers behind sent the glass hurling towards her silver rapper jumpsuit. As the girl went to throw a punch, Heather went into WPC mode and grabbed her from behind and suggested advice in her ear.

'Don't go getting yourself in trouble for that little shit. You can see she's pissed, just calm down yeah.'

She signalled over to the bouncer. The intoxicated girl was then escorted out of the building amongst shouts of approval from the bar queue. She let go of the girl and grabbed her a bar towel to dab herself down.

'I hope she's not a friend of yours—silly cow's gonna get herself slapped real hard if she tries that on the wrong person.'

'No, nothing to do with me. I'm with that plonker over there.'

Gareth was now in full swing with his shirt off and over his head, like some sort of deranged nun. Both girls laughed and pointed at him, but he didn't seem to care.

'I have one of them, too. He's over there asleep in the corner. Bloody gay boys can't hold their liquor like us lezzas. I'm Soraya, but my friends call me Ray. Can I get you a drink?'

Before she knew it, she was up against the wall in the back of the club with her tongue down this random woman with Betty Boop curls and hoop earrings throat. She was too drunk to care and had thrown out any ideas of staying sober.

As soon as the club lights came on, so did hers. She looked for Gareth, only to find him in the same position as her with one of the white T-shirt brigade.

'Gareth, come on Mate, we're leaving.'

After a few attempts, she dragged him off the floor and onto his feet. He was in a worse state than her, so she gave a salute to the girl that was still waiting for her, then bundled him out of the door.

This could work, she thought. They had both witnessed the homophobia that was going on in the college. And had been privy to a few stories from some bigoted officers as they took the piss out of a new female constable that was openly gay. She had felt no gay vibe from Gareth, but looking at him with that boy in the club, it was apparent that this type of involvement had happened before.

The next morning, Gareth and Heather woke up in her bed. They both had little recollection from the night before as they desperately tried to swallow down some paracetamols and flat coke. They were both naked, and that had confused them.

'So did we?—or am I just assuming—oh my God

Heather, I'm so sorry.'

Heather laughed and threw his trousers at him.

'I haven't got a frigging clue, Mate—and do you know what? I don't care.'

They had such a good time last night, and she had enjoyed the wild abandonment. They were a good team and what they did was their business.

Being back on the Beechwood estate and in a police uniform was intimidating for Heather. But she knew that if she wanted to make a difference, the community that she had grown up with side by side would be a good start. She and Gareth worked a lot together. They gave them the petty crimes that the more seasoned officers avoided.

At night, the estate stayed awake. Call-outs from neighbourhood watch teams were a matter of course.

Mainly it was to report vandalism and the odd car being set alight, but this time it was an unusual disturbance at the shopping centre.

The residents living in the maisonettes above reported the sound of screeching birds and what sounded like screaming. As usual, Heather and Gareth were the rookies sent down to investigate.

The smell from the heavily gated toilets hit them on their arrival and as they checked the shutters on the shops' everything seemed intact. Discarded carrier bags were being taken by the wind and the sound of empty coke cans echoed under the stone pillars, but nothing sounded out of place.

As they followed the trail of squashed potato and newspaper all the way to the chip shop, they could hear banging coming from the inside. The little shits had forced the lock on the bottom of the shutter open. As Gareth lifted the metal high into its recess, the screams were deafening.

One boy was constantly shouting 'fuck off' and frantically waving his hands above his head.

Another started pushing on the inside of the door, shouting, 'Let us out, come on hurry.'

Heather shone her torch through the window. Two teenage boys who were covered in what looked like bird shit were running around in circles. Screaming like babies.

As Heather went to open the door, Gareth stopped her. He was in a fit of hysteria, and they carried on watching the chancers.

'Don't open it yet, this is classic.'

They stood back and scoffed at the boys, trying hard to push open the door, that they should have been pulling.

'How long do you think it will take before they realise?'

'God knows.' Heather cupped her hand and squinted closer through the glass. 'Is that pigeons in there with them?'

Gareth gave another outburst of laughter before moving away. 'I'd better take a look around the back and see how they got in. They probably smashed this outside lock for a quick getaway.'

After dodging tins of used oil, he climbed up and into the large metal bins that were full of potato peelings.

As he reached the edge of the guttering, he scraped the sausage and batter that was stuck to the bottom of his shoe off, before carefully climbing onto the roof.

He tapped his torch on his leg to wake up the batteries and noticed a gaping hole in the skylight. Under the extractor fan was a huddle of pigeons annoyed at being disturbed by the raucous. He smirked at the thought of the boys climbing in with that lot flying around their heads, then left them in peace.

Heather gave in and pushed the door from the outside. Three annoyed pigeons flew out, followed by two shit-peppered fourteen-year-olds.

They tried to push past her and run, but Gareth stopped them both in their tracks.

The chip shop had three slot machines, and they were always full of money. Lots of estate kids over the years had attempted to break in. Some were successful, others caught in action. It was a regular coming of age thing.

As they entered the station to file the report, DI Martha Moss grabbed Heather to one side.

'You'll do. Come with me. I've got a little job for you to do.'

This was the first time that Martha had spoken to Heather, and she felt a little excited to be asked. She was too much of a newbie to be noticed by any of the higher-ranking officers and had just accepted her ghost existence around the place. Maybe this could be the start of her career, she thought.

'How are you at getting your hands into small spaces?'

Heather didn't answer, just shrugged before being dragged by the arm through the big double doors and over to a small, battered MG in the car park.

'See, my problem is I've locked my bloody keys in the car, and I can't get my big bloody arms through that small window.'

Heather could see her keys on the passenger seat. She took off her coat and, after rolling up her sleeve, she tried with all her strength to retrieve them through the crack in the window.

'Go on girl, you're nearly there.'

She could feel the window close tightly around her now swollen arm, but no matter how hard she tried to grab them, she was at least two inches away from success.

'OK, OK you can stop. Maybe we need to call out the police to help, hey,' she sneered.

Heather was glad to stop. Her arm had become purple with trying.

As she put her coat back on, she could feel this woman checking her out. Martha was a lot older than her, but she was still a smart-looking woman. She always wore designer suits and wasn't shy of the odd spray tan. Keeping her peppered hair short around a stern but beautiful face made her look as though she knew what she was doing. Not bumbling around like some of the other inspectors that Heather had come into contact with. She had caused quite an effect on her and the smart forty-something had always made Heather's belly flip whenever she came into the station.

'It's Heather, isn't it?' Martha could also feel a mutual attraction and wondered why she had never noticed how beautiful the girl was before.

'Thanks for trying, anyway. I think we need to use more drastic measures.'

She moved towards Heather, who was now leaning on the car. She put her hands on either side of her waist and eased her out of the way. Within seconds, she grabbed for her truncheon and smashed the side window.

Heather jumped at the sound of the breaking glass and hid at the back of Martha as she removed the shards of glass that were refusing to drop to the floor.

'That worked,' she smiled. 'Can you pop inside and grab a dustpan and brush for me Officer? We can't leave all this glass out here.'

Heather nodded and went inside the station to get the brush as quickly as she could. Her heart was beating loudly, and she was feeling the excitement of being in the older woman's presence.

As she went back to the car park, Martha was getting into a police car opposite. She smiled at her and shook her retrieved keys.

'Thanks, Heather, I owe you one.'

She started the car, then pulled up alongside her.

'Can you also tape a bin liner over that open window for me Love, it looks like it's gonna rain later?'

As the car pulled away, Heather's heart dropped. She couldn't say no, as she was way too far down the pecking order to answer back to an officer of her ranking.

The next time she saw Martha, she made sure not to be so gullible. A driver had had his window put through by some kids throwing rocks on the estate. It was becoming a regular occurrence. The bus and taxi drivers had refused to pick up from some areas with fears of hurting their passengers. The police had tried to monitor the area on foot but hadn't yet been lucky enough to catch them at it.

'We have to stop meeting like this amongst the broken glass. It's becoming a habit.'

Heather was quite shocked that Martha had remembered her and blushed in response as Martha continued.'Maybe you'd like to share a bottle of wine or two later when we finish up here?'

All Heather could do was nod her head. The confident young WPC had felt like a quivering wreck around the DI. A drink would be good though, and a way of calming her unsteady nerves.

When Heather walked into the Feathers, several nameless faces that she had seen around the station greeted her. This was a colleague get together and not the intimate night she had hoped for.

She found Martha standing at the bar, laughing with the barmaid. As she approached, she hoped she hadn't forgotten that she had asked her out. Martha's face was inviting and as she waved towards her, she smiled. It wasn't until another DI that was standing behind her greeted Martha first, that she realised the wave wasn't for her. 'How embarrassing' she thought.

She sucked back her shame and pushed her way through to the bar.

'Hey, Heather, you made it. Sorry about the noise. It gets crazy in here with this lot. Look around, you may know some of them.'

'That's OK and yes, I've seen a few of these faces around the station.'

Martha nodded and got the crowd's attention.

'Listen up guys, this is Heather.' The embarrassment made her want to crawl under the bar. The guys greeted her in unison with nods and waves.

'She's getting a round in, so what are you having?'

As soon as the words fell from her lips, a wave of hands lifted their glasses and the barmaid took their order.

Heather went into her purse to pay for the drinks, but Martha stopped her.

'I was only joking. Most of this lot are on pints with whiskey chasers you would be skint until next payday.'

Heather felt relieved. She was still paying off her catalogue and didn't have that much cash to spare. Martha handed the barmaid a fifty-pound note and took her whiskey, and Heather's wine, to a quiet table.

The conversation was freely flowing, and after her third glass, Heather was feeling at ease with the woman.

'So, Martha, how did you bypass these guys to get to the top? I've heard it's pretty hard to get a promotion unless you're an exceptional officer.'

Martha smiled and leaned in towards Heather.

'That must be what I am then.' She leaned in a little more. 'You need to play the game and let them think that they have the upper hand. Keep your nose clean and tell them what they want to hear. When it's your time to shine, you'll know about it, then all you have to do is make sure everyone else does too.' She leaned back and downed the last of her whiskey. 'We are strong women Heather If you get things done the right way, you can make yourself indispensable to these guys. Trust me.'

She unhooked her jacket from the side of the chair and swirled it around her shoulders.

'Right, that's me done. I'll catch up with you again, yeah?'

Heather didn't want to be sitting there on her own, so asked her to wait while she popped to the ladies for them to walk out together. Martha took this as an invitation and followed her in.

When Heather came out of the cubicle, Martha was waiting. She had a look of wanting in her eyes and gently moved in for a kiss from Heather. As they both went back in, Martha locked the door behind her.

They were about to get to know each other better when Martha's phone went off. She had to stop and take the call, as the case she was working on meant she was never off duty. Unlucky for them, they had called her back into the station and there was no time to lose. The unplanned rendezvous was over. They exchanged personal numbers to arrange a date at the weekend. Heather was happy. She would go home and dream of what might have been and what might be in store.

The weekend came and went and still no sign of Martha. Heather worried that she may have forgotten about her. She was always the one being chased, so making the first move was not something she had ever had to do. She had heard a few rumours about Martha from the boys at the station but had ignored them until now. They were always assuming that because Martha was a lesbian, she would pursue every woman she came in contact with. She hoped that wasn't the case and left a quick, nonchalant message on her answering machine.

When Martha did eventually respond, she invited her to a meal at her place. It was nothing special but would be a lot cheaper if she were to be called away than if they had gone to an expensive restaurant.

After the food, Heather had planned to go straight home, but Martha insisted they had one more drink together in front of the open fire. The heat had the desired effect and Heather was feeling relaxed as they sat on the fake fur rug.

'You don't have to leave. Do you? I was looking forward to getting to know you better.'

Martha leaned in and kissed Heather's neck. The belly flip she was so used to having every time she saw Martha was now more of a cartwheel. Without control, she felt her body respond, aching to feel her touch. She lifted her head and found Martha's warm lips. Small soft kisses gave way to hard, sweet caresses. Martha's kisses trailed between Heather's breasts as she slowly undid her buttons. Her skin, glistening from the heat, had made her want her even more. As she continued to undress her, Heather lifted Martha's shirt over her head. Her hard nipples teased through her black sports bra. Heather groaned as Martha climbed onto her naked body. Begging her to explore the passion she had created by taking her to limits that only another woman could reach.

When Heather awoke, Martha had gone. She left a note saying, 'help yourself to breakfast and lock the door on the way out'.

She found a shirt of Martha's and put it on her sleek body. She loved the way it smelled of Martha.

The house was quite basic and as she perused the photos on the walls with a cup of coffee in her hand; she thought of Gareth. They had been getting on well lately, and he had suggested that maybe they get married to hide away from a homophobic existence.

She was seriously considering it, but now she had Martha to think about. She wondered if her being married may make any difference to their relationship.

When she got to the station, Martha was there. She walked over to her and gently touched her hand before making her way to the front desk. Martha looked up and looked away. Heather had wanted to wrap her legs around her in a big, good morning hug, but the woman barely acknowledged the fact that she was there. There was a stern look on her face and not one that she had noticed before. She thought that after spending the night together, Martha may have had a slight glow about her. But as she looked over to Heather, there was no hint of requited love.

It was lunchtime before Martha made the move to talk to her.

'Was everything OK when you left? You locked up, OK?'

'Yeah, of course—last night was amazing. Maybe we could do it again sometime, yeah?'

Martha looked at her and gave a half-smile. 'You know we get really busy here Heather, so I don't have time for committed relationships.'

Heather stopped her in mid-sentence.

'God no, I'm not into committed relationships either.'

Martha smiled and was happy that Heather was on the same page as her.

'It's not like we can't see each other again, though, you know. As long as we both understand what's going on here.'

Heather nodded her head and in the back of her mind, she knew exactly what Martha had wanted. This was how the rumour mongers around the station had described her, 'Just like one of the boys.' Love, then leave them—until the next time she needed a quick fuck.

On the day of their wedding, the new soon to be Heather Williams received a phone call from her boss Martha. Even though she had never wanted commitment, she had been trying to talk her out of marrying Gareth. As much to her own annoyance, she had spent many a night in Martha's bed despite knowing what she was like. This time she was thinking of herself. It was OK for Martha. She had already climbed the ladder, regardless of her sexuality. She had gained respect from a lot of the men as she would probably beat them hands down in a fistfight.

Heather didn't have the same appeal that Martha had. Her appearance made the men ask her for her phone number not to be the backup on a stakeout or anything. If she was to even attempt to climb the same ladder as Martha, she needed a different tactic. Being a woman loving woman would not open doors for her.

Heather was adamant not to make her sexuality public, and marrying Gareth was the only way to keep it under wraps from her family and work colleagues. There had been too many girls being side-lined and unnoticed when promotion time came around. If they knew she was also a lesbian, the door would be well and truly bolted.

The world was not ready to see gays and lesbians in positions of power, and the police force had its own policies against any promotion.

She had heard of a colleague that Gareth had been seeing who came out to their senior officer. As soon as he did, they suspended him for three days. The officer in charge said, 'he couldn't condone his actions as a homosexual and would have to re-evaluate his position within the force.' There was also a request sent to the powers that be, about moving him. The senior officer worried that the rest of the team may victimise him, so advised the mixed-race officer to act more like a white straight man.

There were a lot of crimes being committed against the gay community and couples taking part in male sex acts were being sort and actively arrested. This had broken Gareth as a few times he had had to arrest friends of his that he could not tip off beforehand.

Gareth was also one of the first officers on the scene after a young gay man had been left for dead at Newport train station. He was on his way home from a night at the King's Cross in Cardiff and had been jumped by three middle-aged men. The CCTV footage had recorded the boy being dragged from a bench and onto the floor while the men continually kicked him and stamped on his head. They later took him to the Royal Gwent Hospital where they questioned him on how he thought he could get away with being alone in Newport, dressed so flamboyantly.

Gareth followed the ambulance with another two officers in the car. The conversation coming from the back seat made Gareth feel sick. They made jokes about the boy's feminine appearance and they both agreed that if you were going to dress like that; you deserved all you got. They never once referred to him by his name and only as poof or queer.

This was all too much for Gareth and Heather. Homophobia was well and truly still alive and to be openly gay and a member of her majesty's police force was not the best position to be in.

They brought the wedding forward. This would be the only way they could protect their secret identities. Masquerading as a loving couple would not be completely impossible, as they loved each other. They also shared a bed and had drunken sex from time to time.

Martha had pulled herself through the ranks by sheer hard work. She was too gutsy and clever at her job to be messed with. Heather knew she needed to toughen herself up if she was ever to walk in Martha's shoes. But with the females outnumbered by one female on a shift of seven, this would be a challenge to get herself noticed, let alone stand out.

The wedding had been a simple registry office affair that they invited only close friends and family to.

The honeymoon was a week in London, and they couldn't wait to get away and just be themselves.

Chapter Two

1999

London was manic and exciting. As soon as they stepped off the train, they watched how people from every colour, nationality and sexual persuasion went about their normal lives commuting about the city. Heather's mum, had tried to talk them out of it. There had been two bomb attacks in the city over the last few weeks. She didn't want them caught up in the aftermath or getting involved in any political goings-on. The newlyweds just brushed it off. They accused her of being overprotective and reminded her that being police officers; they were used to living on the edge of danger. Patrolling the Beechwood estate was much scarier than a week in London could ever be.

They found a bed-and-breakfast in Brixton. It was a lot cheaper and close enough to the tube station to get in and out of the central quickly. The owner of the house seemed a bit of a windbag and asked them a lot of questions. She spouted off the rules of the house with her strong Jamaican accent as soon as they stepped through the door.

Gareth put their suitcase on the bed and started opening the cupboards, looking for hangers to put up his new collection of tight T-shirts and even tighter fitting jeans. He had never felt comfortable wearing anything like this at home. Instead, he wore jackets with patches on the elbows and corduroy trousers which he hated. The only real thing he wore every day was his Freddie moustache. He vowed never to shave it off, no matter how much stick he received about it. Here would be different. He could be the real him.

He had thought of wearing his Frankie says relax t-shirt from the 80s, but Heather had told him that would be going too far.

'So what time are we meeting them?'

'I told Ray that I'd call her when we arrived. Calm down, it will be OK.'

Soraya had become a close friend after their first meeting at Club X. She had been out most weekends that Heather had, and they had spent a few nights together.

When Heather and Gareth told her they were spending the week in London, she promised to meet up with them.

Brixton was Soraya's hometown, and all her family still lived there. She had moved to Cardiff originally with a girlfriend, but when it didn't work out, she stayed in the city because of her job. She still came back at least once a month to visit her family and always met up with her old drinking crew. These friends would be perfect for Heather and Gareth. They could showcase queer London and give them a damn good time doing it.

They had kept the details of their relationship on a need-to-know basis. Police officers, married to each other to hide their true identities, may not pass as exactly honest. Only someone in the same situation could ever understand how a fake honeymoon could mean everything to them. They were posing as work colleagues from nine-to-five office jobs. Simple and boring enough not to be questioned about.

'Are you sure that she said it was OK for me to tag along? I don't want to be a spare part.'

'Gareth, you could never be a spare part you are too much of a tool for that. I told you she has lots of friends that are guys. Maybe you'll meet the man of your dreams.'

'Man of my nightmares, more like after seeing the plonkers in Cardiff that she hangs around with.'

It was a warm April and even though it was the middle of the week; it was still heaving in all the clubs and bars. After eating lunch while walking around the usual tourist traps, they were ready to meet up with Soraya.

The pub was the Old Compton in Soho. The place was full of people having a good time. It was nothing like Newport or Cardiff, even. People looked free to be themselves.

As they walked in, posters of drag queen shows greeted them. Black and white photos of lesbians and gay men dancing together at what looked like the speakeasies from the early days were around every corner. London had been notorious in the past for its underground queer bars. Even though you had to be a member to enter, they were continually being found out and closed down. Arrests and hard labour could only be avoided if the patrons promised never to frequent places like that again. Although, some would stand their ground and imprisonment was imminent.

As they approached the bar, there was an oldish man in a pink dressing gown patting a white fluffy dog who sat on a stool in the corner. He smiled at them and carried on drinking his wine spritzer. The barman was a young handsome Latino looking lad and Gareth immediately felt like they had made the right decision.

They took their drinks to an outside table and watched as Soraya and another two friends bent down to greet them on arrival.

'I can't believe you made it. I thought that you two were a bit too square for this sort of thing, with your safe little office jobs.'

She pulled up a seat next to them and hung her jacket on the side of the chair.

'This is Peter and his new friend, Sean. He's like you two. He's only been in London a couple of weeks after moving here from Ireland.'

The boys gave air kisses and went off inside to get drinks.

'So, tell me, what do you think so far? It's a lot different from Wales, isn't it?'

Before Heather could answer, Soraya continued.

'Gareth, are you OK? You look a bit lost in thought, Mate.'

He smiled and downed his bottle. He *was* feeling lost. In front of him were openly gay couples kissing and enjoying being themselves. He didn't want to seem leary, but he couldn't take his eyes off them. Heather knew that this would hit Gareth harder than her. He had this hard man cop image to uphold at home when sometimes all he wanted to do was chill out in his pyjamas, watching episodes of Will and Grace.

'I know all this seems strange at first, but you will get used to it, I promise.'

Soraya smiled, and all seemed well with the world. It was as if they were in a parallel universe. This is how it should be they both felt. These cloak and dagger fake wedding ideas were a means to an end, but in their real world, both would have liked nothing more than to be accepted for who they were. Both bisexual, and both happy in their own choices.

When the boys came back to the table, Sean sat next to Gareth. His reactions were the same as his. His eyes darted around everywhere, taking in this surreal place where people were just people and not freaks of nature.

'Gareth, I know exactly how you feel, Mate. I'm from Northern Ireland and back there they would arrest me for just being gay, let alone kissing in public. They find any excuse to throw you in jail.' He was quite a rugged-looking young man and not the type that Gareth would have thought of as gay if he didn't know.

'So, are you living here now then, Sean?'

'I have no choice, Mate. I can't go back.'

Peter butted in at this point and put his arm around Sean.

'We wouldn't let you go back, anyway. You're one of us now.' He gently placed a kiss on the top of his head, then slapped him across it. 'He just needs to loosen up a bit or he'll never find himself a shag.'

Sean blushed with embarrassment. He still hadn't kissed a boy, as he was still self-shaming behind the fear, driven into him in Northern Ireland.

He grew up with the Ian Paisley 'Save Ulster from Sodomy campaign', of which his parents were active members. When he was younger, they had used him for pushing leaflets through doors. He had to stand proudly next to them as they shouted anti-gay slogans across loudspeakers. It took him a long time to accept his sexuality and after three failed suicide attempts, he accepted he could no longer live a lie, so moved to London.

Peter had been helping with the Gay switchboard and was also the face of the gay men's support group. After assuring him he was not a freak, they got him a place to stay and a part-time job at the office.

Later that night, they met up and hit the clubs. London's gay scene was a total culture shock, filled with the most flamboyant drag queens and kings that they had ever seen. People of all ages, shapes, and sizes, were just out for a good time. The music was a mixture of high energy dance and cheesy pop classics. They danced the night away, and for once, they felt normal.

When Friday came, they were planning for the weekend. It was a bank holiday, so everywhere was going to be packed. Gareth had been to Camden market earlier with Peter and Sean, and they had bought the most outrageous pink feather bowers to strut around for the night. When he got back to the bed-and-breakfast he still had it around his neck. The old lady rolled her eyes at him and sucked through her teeth before muttering her disapproval.

'Men used to dress as men in my day. Not parading around town like Nancy boys.'

They were to meet up at 6 pm in the Admiral Duncan pub in Soho. It was another warm day, and they couldn't wait to down a couple of early evening beers. For the first time in a long time, they were feeling comfortable in their own skins. On the way, they toyed with the idea of them moving to London for good. They could have a divorce party and a coming-out party on the same day.

They made their way to Dean Street and just before they turned the corner onto Old Compton Street, a deafening bang abused the bustle of taxi horns and street noise. Just for a few seconds, it was silent. As they walked on to Old Compton Street, it met them with a wall of smoke. An acrid smell of charred flesh and heavy dust filled their nostrils.

Visibility was poor. Out of the smoke, people were running to get as far away from the explosion as possible. One man was shouting, telling everyone to turn around and get the hell out of there. Others were just shouting

'Bomb.'

It was Friday 30th April 1999 and a nail bomb had gone off inside the Admiral Duncan pub.

As Gareth and Heather realised what had happened, they ran towards the scene and not away from it. This was what her parents were trying to warn them about. There had already been two previous bombs; one in Brixton and one in Brick Lane. The police had mentioned that they had thought they were racist attacks, so Soho's gay district was not a cause for concern.

There was glass and blood everywhere. The pub had had its doors blown clean off. Amongst the debris, bodies were many. Some not moving, some screaming in agony. After composing themselves, they both looked desperately through them to see if they could find their friends. They helped those out of the building that they could and sat them on the rubble outside. They both noticed Peter at the same time. He was sitting with his back against a pile of broken chairs, with his head in his hands. They approached him with care as not to startle him, but as soon as he saw them, he tried to stand. He held on to Heather, desperately trying to pull himself up.

'You've got to help Sean. I tried, I really did, but I couldn't pull him out.'

As he turned to face them, it was visible that his left ear was missing, along with the side of his face. What he had left of his eye, was streaming with blood and he was dropping in and out of consciousness in front of them.

The screams from the sirens were now drowning out the pitiful wailing from the injured. Peter had stopped breathing. Heather lay him on the ground and tried not to disturb the four-inch nails that were embedded into his skin. She resuscitated him and brought him back just before a paramedic took over.

As Gareth turned to look for the others, he noticed the white fluffy dog from the Old Compton, pulling on what looked like the tie from a pink dressing gown. As he got closer, he could see his owner trapped under a pile of heavy tables. The dog's bark had alerted two of the bar staff that had made it out unscathed, so he carried on with his own pursuit to find the others.

Visibility was still very poor as the dust had not yet fully settled. As he made his way over the debris, he stood on a shoe that still had a foot inside. He moved it to a safer place, giving it the respect it deserved. Under a pile of wood and concrete, he saw Sean. He called out to him and his face flickered acknowledgement; he was still alive.

The concrete blocks were heavy. His hands were sweaty as he tried endlessly to get a good grip on them. Finally, he could see what he was dealing with and after digging away with bloody knuckles he freed his new friend. Both of his legs were missing from the knee down and he was losing a lot of blood. Gareth tried to stem the flow by wrapping his jacket around the raw flesh while calling out for help. His shouts were not in vain, and a young firefighter came to Gareth's side. After a few stumbling attempts trawling over rubble and body parts, they carried Sean out.

Everyone was still in a state of shock and panic. Someone had suggested that there may be another bomb, and people were clambering over one another to get out.

Outside, missing arms and legs were strewn onto upturned tables. People were crying out, trying to find their friends. Everyone knew that this was not an accident.

But no one had expected it to be an attack against the gay community.

As Heather and Gareth tried to assist the wounded, they noticed Soraya stumbling from the pub. She was in complete shock and her bottom lip was trembling.

''I saw the poster on the pub toilet door. It said ''Bombs Beware''. We were just talking about it.'' She put her hands through her dust-filled fro and continued in tears. 'There was a rucksack on the floor and we both said that it looked suspicious. Me and Sean were sitting right next to it. If I hadn't gone down to the jukebox, I'd be in a billion pieces by now.' The realisation hit her. 'Oh, my fucking God, where are the boys?'

She spun around in circles in complete panic. Heather reached out and grabbed her with both arms; held her tight to stop her shaking. 'It's OK, they are both out.'

She didn't want to say any more than that, as she wasn't sure whether either of them would make it. Both men's injuries were horrific.

A few weeks later, it was all over the news that they had caught the bomber. He was a twenty-two-year-old Neo-Nazi and had admitted to being racist and homophobic. This was his reason for the attacks. The hate that had grown inside this young mind had damaged the once free gay community of Soho and, along with a few bystanders that had laughed in the faces of the injured many, the world once again was a very unsafe and unacceptable place to be.

After making sure that their friends were getting all the help that they needed, the newlyweds had to return home. They had already taken an extra week of unpaid leave each and had explained to their boss that they were helping with what had happened in Soho. No one assumed their involvement as they were on their honeymoon. They accepted their story of them just passing by when the bomb went off as truth.

They had helped their community as much as they could by parading as police officers from another country. Before that, they had spent time in an idyllic world that had had its entire existence crushed by one man. They were now back behind closed doors, hiding a love that would always be of the wrong kind.

Life would carry on as its kind of normal for now and Mr and Mrs Williams accepted their new lives together as a team. One loving the other, in a relationship that was always open to suggestion.

Chapter Three

2009

Thick curls of smoke ascended from under the storeroom door. Luckily for Mike Hayden, he had caught sight of it before locking the yard for the weekend. He tanked around the back and after rubbing the dirt from the pane; he cupped his hands on the tiny window, squinting to focus. Amongst the reams of pure white paper was a burning bin full of rubbish, throwing its flames around to tease the flammable contents that were sitting high on the shelves.

'Bloody estate kids,' he snarled. The only working fire extinguisher was under the desk, and he cracked his head hard as he squeezed his colossal frame into the small space to grab it. It was just enough to dowse the flames, and he coughed along with the extra smoke he had now created. He wiped the sweat from his brow and looked back out into the yard. He could see the hooded chancers with cans of spray paint defacing the back of the trucks. He threw the extinguisher to the floor and clambered over the sodden aftermath before bounding through the door.

'Oi ya little bastards…' clutching his chest, he gave chase. It was too much for the old man. His running days were over. Being overweight and overworked saw pay for that. He shouted again and forced one foot in front of the other, but they were too fast and had dodged him—again. After shaking his fist in the air at nothing, he made it back inside and wheezed as he slumped himself onto his half-peeled leather chair to catch his breath.

The kids ran out of the haulage yard and over to the black Lexus that was waiting for them on the corner. After tapping on the window, a hand came out with a ten-pound note in its fingers. The tallest of the boys took the money from the driver, then they climbed the railings and ran off across the field with cheeky smiles on their dirty faces.

Behind the black tinted windows sat two of Frankie Thompson's henchmen. Steve, the better looking of the two, was checking his teeth in the vanity mirror. The nasty one, Vic, shook his head at him and looked at his watch.

'We'll give the old bastard ten minutes, then we'll pay him a visit.'

After lifting the remains of the fire into the skip, Mike held the bottom of his back and felt it crack under his hand. He had wanted to get out early so he could sink a few whiskeys before going home to his needy brood, but that would not happen now. His wife would be there with her list of demands orchestrated by his grown-up children that were too lazy to get jobs of their own and relied on him for everything.

As he walked back into the office, Vic greeted him in his heavy black leather jacket and hands the size of shovels wafting the air in front of his face.

'It's a bit hot in here Hayden,' he pretended to cough with his deep gravel voice. 'What you been up to then—cooking the books?'

Vic walked over to Mike Hayden's desk and perched himself on the end of it. He rummaged around on the top and tore open the pack of limp service-station cheese sandwiches that Mike hadn't had time to eat.

'You don't want these do you fatty?'

The old man felt the shirt on his back fill with sweat and stick to him as he tried to not let the man know that he intimidated him.

'No, you carry on—you're going to anyway,' he said under his breath.

'What was that?' He sprawled at the man with a full mouthful before waving the half-eaten sandwich in his face. 'It's getting too hot for you in here, Hayden' he sniggered at his pun. 'Isn't it about time you realise you need protection?'

Mike Hayden was scared, but the anger that was boiling in him made him show his irritation at the man and he shook his head. Vic lunged at him and was about to give him a quick slap before being interrupted by the sound of a forklift in the yard. He smiled at the old man with the grease of the sandwich shining on his chin'.

'That will be my mate, Steve.'

Mike Hayden managed to loosen himself from his grip and ran into the yard.

The forklift had been scraping the sides of the pallets of paper scoring into their shrink-wrap coverings. He called out to stop him and started waving his hands to catch the attention of the driver. Steve smiled then drove the truck at him, pinning him against the wall between the forks.

The old man squeezed his portly shape under his metal captor and hoping to make it to his car he darted out, but Vic was waiting for him.

'Naughty boy,' he tutted. 'You can't run from us, Mate.'

The men carted him back to the office and pushed him onto the floor. Vic knelt by the side of him, patting his balding head.

'I told you this would happen, Hayden—all you had to do was pay up.'

The old man gritted his teeth in reply, 'You want me to pay for protection when the only thing I need protecting from is you.' His breathing was getting heavy, and he was having trouble trying to hold his head up.

'After the last time you ignored us, I told you that if you didn't want our services, then you would have to prove that you're a big enough force to be reckoned with; and here you are snivelling at me to let you go.'

Both men took an underarm each and raised him off the floor. He was heavy, and they complained about the sweat that the old man was profusely secreting before dropping him into his chair. Steve thought it would be fun to spin the old man around a few times before watching him spew all over himself.

Mike Hayden was finding it hard to focus, but as Steve took a blade out of his pocket and cleaned his nails with it, the shine from the steel caught his eye.

'The thing is, Mike, there are a lot of bad people out there—you can't trust anyone these days—and my boss, well, he's worried about you. He doesn't want you to suffer.'

The old man could feel the tightness return in his chest as the sweat dripped down his face. He reached into his pocket for his tablets, but as soon as Vic caught sight of them, he knocked them out of his hand.

'Oh, dear Mike, it's not another heart attack like last year, is it?' he picked up the tablets and shook them in the old man's face. 'All this pressure is not good for you. Let's say you pay me a grand now out of that tin over there and I'll ask Steve to clean his nails outside.'

The old man's breathing was becoming shallow, and he whispered his words, 'I have got no money to spare. My family is bleeding me dry as it is.' The pain in his chest had gotten worse and had travelled down his left arm. 'Please—please leave me alone…'

He fell onto the floor clutching at his chest and the boys laughed at him. Vic went back to the desk and took the other sandwich out of its packet. He munched away at it while watching the man struggle with his breathing. He looked over at Steve, who was staring at him.

'What—I've had no lunch. He's not gonna eat it, is he?'

As Mike Hayden took his last breaths, the boys lifted him back onto his office chair. They began idly chatting about visiting the bookies as the man tried in vain to grab the inches of life he had left in him. As the last breath finally took, he thumped his head onto his desk.

Vic wiped his dirty mouth on his sleeve and took out his mobile.

'Ramsey—You can tell Frankie Thompson it's done.'

Chapter Four

Hayden Haulage had been a trusted family business for over fifty years, until the old man died, taking his life experience with him. Mike Hayden was the last in the line of hands-on grafters, leaving behind a family of squawking birds worrying that their nest would soon lose its feathers.

After giving him a modest funeral, they flapped around with their perfectly manicured hands, anxious that their comfortable lifestyles were about to change. The greedy accountants had advised them to seek outside help. They needed a general manager to take them under their wing. Within a few days, a hurried advertisement went out in all the local papers. They received many applicants and had whittled them down to just a few.

As James Hayden waited in his late father's office for the candidates to arrive, he perched on the edge of the chair as not to get his expensive suit dirty.

In the reception room next door, two prospective candidates waited anxiously to be seen. The older of the two men was looking down his nose at the younger one as if to insinuate that his years of experience would surely get him the job. But the younger man, who was relying on his technical knowledge, didn't play to his intimidating glances. They both sat in comfort with their abilities, glancing at the clock and checking their watches. It was nearly one o'clock, and they were both glad to be the only candidates.

As Bill Ramsgate entered with Vic and Steve in tow, both men suddenly felt inferior. This was supposed to be a job interview, not a muscle contest, the older man thought. Bill Ramsgate stood in the middle of the floor, clapped his hands, then rubbed them together. He smiled at the candidates in turn, before making his announcement.

'Right then, lads, if one of you could shut the door on your way out, it would be much appreciated.'

The two men stared at each other for a second, not knowing quite what was happening, until Vic and Steve kindly helped them on their way.

Ramsgate came with shiny recommendations, reeling in the family's trust and allowing them to breathe again. His sanctimonious sales pitch showed his charm and driving force. They thought him perfect to be the new spearhead for the company as he bowled them over with his ideas to propel Hayden Haulage into the 21st century. By the time his interview had finished, it left James Hayden feeling as if Ramsgate would do them a favour by joining the company. So he accepted him and his fake Armani suit with no more questions asked.

His people skills were also to be admired. He used his trusting smile embedded with an excellent set of teeth to become an instant hit with the workforce. The promise of overtime and extra money to be made with a cash in hand wink, was lapped up by the struggling family men and their out of hand debts.

The company soon expanded, and Ramsgate's charm was proving its worth. The drivers felt appreciated with their new lorries; sciatica was no longer the major cause for absence. The extra hoists and pulleys replaced muscle spasms. Specialist transportation equipment to ferry the rolls of paper all over Europe for their most loyal customer, 'Paper by Kings', saw more orders coming in. Mutual profits increased, and everyone was happy.

The family felt back in the arms of a parent. They were also pleased to hear that in such a brief space of time, Ramsgate had doubled the business load by securing another prestigious customer. This suited everyone, especially Ramsgate. He would sit back in Mike's old chair with his hands on his head, smiling to himself. Soon all of his hard work would pay off; fulfilling his dreams of grandeur.

'Starling Prestige' was as prestigious as Fagin's school for boys. It was headed by the Beechwood estate gangster Frankie Thompson, notorious for cultivating schemes to perfection. Now, in his sixties, he had earned the respect from the lowest kind of scum Newport had to offer. If there was an inside job happening, you could guarantee that it was one of his men guarding the gate.

He stopped working on the ground floor years ago. The police had his name as a suspect for a lot of dirty dealings, but without any hard evidence, they could never make it stick.

Back in 2000, he had played a different hand and received ten years at Cardiff Prison for inciting gangland murders. He had become trigger-happy by proxy and sought revenge for his brand new BMW'S demise, chalked up by the Canton clan wielding metal poles. The embarrassment had unglued him, and he started taking chances with loose lips.

Without his usual scrutiny, he made the mistake of spitting his bile to an undercover cop by parading £10k in front of him. He insisted it was on offer to anyone that would stiff a member of the rival gang. When things didn't go to plan and his pawns were getting themselves wiped out, he emerged from his safe house to see justice done. Thompson only pulled the trigger to threaten once, but that was enough to bring him down. This taught him a vital lesson and from then on, he never got his hands dirty and exonerated himself at every opportunity.

Ramsgate, then known as 'Ramsey,' had bunked up with Frankie when he was in for two years for fraud. The old gangster had seen quite a coterie of fraudsters in his time inside. And Ramsey's art of conning those too stupid to see it had impressed him. Whilst unwinding at her majesty's pleasure, they seemed to have found in each other the perfect cellmate. They enjoyed picking each other's brains. Their criminal minds worked in sync as they concocted a scheme that would make them millions.

When they were both still inside, they put their feelers out amongst the white-collar nasties; looking to manipulate an unforeseen opportunity. It took some time but eventually, Hayden Haulage was flagged up with everything they needed apart from one insignificant problem, old man Hayden. They had their tainted accountants search for any weaknesses to gnaw away at within the running of the company, but drew a blank. The only way they would get inside was to create some weaknesses of their own.

Ramsgate had led the gullible Hayden family to believe that 'Starling Prestige' was a growing paper mill. They would be using their haulage services to send their paper to Germany to have a special treatment applied before returning to the UK for finishing. Ramsgate received a pat on the back after he announced they had chosen Hayden Haulage over their competitors with the company's entire transport contract. He conveniently held back the real secrets hidden away amongst the reams of white. They filled the lorries with extra compartments; a maze of hidden levers positioning themselves out of reach from the uneducated eye. The money laundering that was now taking place and the counterfeit production of twenty-pound notes that were being produced were taking care of their own anonymity. Hiding away like children in a game of hide and seek.

Ramsgate manipulated the figures on both accounts. He trod on a few of the smaller customers that old man Hayden had kept on out of loyalty to make time for the new business. They were no good to him and he forced them out by putting the prices up, making their services impossible to afford. But, as long as the company continued to thrive in the eyes of the family, details of lost loyalty didn't seem to matter. He played to their greed and conned them into letting him take on a batch of new drivers. They rubbed their hands together when he told them how their profits would increase.

Frankie had been happy to sit in the background and watch their plan unfold. It had been a long time coming but was worth the wait. After his prison release, it didn't take him long to rebuild his empire. His reputation had only been hardened by his time inside, and he still had enough minions throwing coats over puddles for him. A lot had changed since his criminal reign. The popularity of the internet was now making things easier to scam people. You didn't have to be there in person, it was easy money.

With more time on his hands, he had taken his eye away from the bigger picture. His restlessness had dragged him by the neck to places that even he couldn't afford.

Gambling with the big boys had him losing the money that Ramsgate was generating for him, hand over fist. His age and the extra pounds he had put on made him sweat more; messing up his poker face.

After losing a cool £10k at cards, he decided he needed more spending power so summoned Vic and Steve. Ramsgate would have to do better. He couldn't keep his hard man image up without a full wallet.

'Get the car. I'm gonna have a word with Ramsey.'

The BMW pulled in front of the casino and the big man got in. He had spent all the money that Ramsey had brought for him, and it still wasn't enough.

As he pulled into the yard, he could see that an advertisement with old man Hayden's face on it had been defaced by kids. This made him smile as they drove down to the office.

Ramsgate was sitting at the desk, desperately shuffling paper around as soon as he came in.

'Trying to look busy. Are we Ramsey?'

'Frankie, how good to see you, Mate.' The two men shook hands over-enthusiastically. 'So, what do I owe the pleasure? You rarely pay me a visit unless you've run out of money. You haven't run out of money already, have you?' he scoffed.

'So, what if I have, it's got fuck all to do with you Buddy boy?'

Frankie looked as though he was about to punch him clean in the face. As he got closer, he kept eye contact with him, lifted his arm, and patted him on the back.

'Stop your whinging Ramsey, you big girl's blouse. I've got an idea.'

Bound by the fears of losing everything, Frankie had talked himself into taking the game up to a dangerous level with greed rewiring his rational mind. He had concluded that twenty-pound notes were for petty criminals and wanted to try his hand at the fifties. Ramsgate's reaction when told was one of disbelief.

'We discussed this at the very beginning, Mate, and you said so yourself that everybody checks a fifty at least twice. Besides, they would be harder to forge and to distribute.'

'Well, I've changed my mind. We've done a good job so far at keeping the pigs off our backs. But you could do better at keeping me happy, Ramsey, us being such good mates, like.'

Ramsey got on the phone to the printing outfit they were using in Germany, and they were not too pleased with the change around of business. When Ramsgate told Frankie of their unwillingness to comply, he exploded. He ordered him like an unruly child to get back on the phone and to make sure they knew who they were dealing with. He told him to point out to them they weren't some Mickey Mouse outfit and if anyone tried to overrule them, they would know about it. Eventually, he spat down the phone himself, warning them that if they didn't do the job, he would send a team of muscle to their factory and have their fucking fingers put in a press with the Queen's head tattooed on them for effect.

Ramsgate swallowed hard and advised him to tread carefully. Things were getting heated. He explained they had to stay with this firm as they were the only ones that could produce the same quality paper as a UK note; using the correct mix of cotton fibre and linen rag to achieve the best outcome.

Frankie started mentioning using the other fraudsters around, especially in Poland.

This made Ramsgate's arse twitch. He tried to talk Frankie out of the idea. He used the adage 'you can't make a silk purse out of a sow's ear' to steer him away. Then explained to him in layman's terms that they were using Bible paper, so their notes didn't feel as genuine as the German ones.

The logistics went over Frankie's head as the greed outweighed his common sense.

He ignored the advice. No, Poland would be where they would make their millions and Ramsgate would have to make it happen.

'Just get it sorted.' He walked around the back of him and whispered in his ear. 'Cos if you don't, I might have to sell this useless little body of yours as spare parts.' Frankie knew that if he didn't sort out his finances soon, this may happen to him as well. So the need was dire. He told him to get over to Poland and not come back until a deal was in place.

Ramsgate bit away at the skin on the bottom of his lip, as the sweat dripped down the side of his cheek. After waiting for the back end of the car to disappear, he let out a disgruntled roar. He knew all about the cheaper company as he had his own side deal of twenties being printed by them.

He had made a separate deal with Phil Jenkins, a seasoned driver for Hayden Haulage to produce some fakes of their own. Phil was not one of Frankie's men, but he knew the man who was making the printing plates for them. They were both aware of the danger and very often had to change their plans at the last minute, sweating in their shoes, so afraid of being caught out by Frankie. If he had found out that they had been taking a few rolls of the good paper over to Poland for printing and to have the metal strips fitted at a cheaper price, they would both be on the missing person's list by now.

Both men worked tirelessly in their dual roles. Phil was a family man and not the type to have naturally involved himself with fraud at this level.

While away, Frankie received a complaint from the team that was inserting the metal strips. They had noticed that some of the printing was looking a little dull. He ordered a batch of rolls to be sent over to him at his home so he could check the quality of the printing for himself. Ramsgate and Jenkins knew nothing about the request. They had both gone to Poland to clear up their mess. Unfortunately, Sid, one of Ramsgate's bent drivers, took the call and chose random rolls from Jenkins' lorry to take to Frankie Thompson's house.

When he arrived, he placed them on top of Frankie's professional size pool table and unwound them. A vein pumped visibly in Frankie's forehead as the notes appeared with their metal strips already in place. He looked over at Sid and clenched his teeth before clicking his fingers for his henchmen to come to his side. The silence of a few seconds had the driver unable to form any words, causing Frankie to go ballistic. He started throwing things around, accusing the driver of trying to finish and distribute the money himself. The driver tried to explain that it wasn't his load, but it fell on betrayed ears. The big man dropped to his knees and pleaded with Frankie, but it was no good. He gave him the smile of a psychopath and told him his fate. He would inject him with an overdose of heroin, before throwing him into the River Usk. This would be the blueprint for anyone that dared to cross him. Nobody made a fool out of Frankie and lived to regret it.

When in Poland, Ramsgate and Phil had told their contacts that under no condition should they have any private dealings with Frankie Thompson, or they would drop them in the shit right up to their necks. Luckily for them, they stuck to their side of the bargain.

As time went on, Frankie became more dubious about everyone's actions and played his cards even closer to his chest. Ramsgate had become a visible wreck, and Frankie worried that there was more to his disapproval of the fifty's than just the added risk factor. Bigger fry had tried to dupe him in the past and not succeeded. He could tell when someone was trying to steer him.

After losing more money at the casino, he hammered home that his decision was the right one.

Everyone would have to comply or suffer the consequences. After added pressure, the German company heeled to his threats and even offered him a cheaper price for the paper. Frankie would have his way.

Ramsgate was right to worry about the changeover. When the printing plates for the new fifty-pound notes were ready, it made the price of everything go up, especially life. Anyone found even thinking about skimming any fifties from the top of the pile would get an instant dismissal from life and be just another name on the missing person's list. Security was becoming a problem for Frankie, as he had lost his trust in everyone, especially Ramsey. The pair were always at each other's throats, wondering if the next customer, through the door, would be the police. Either that or a gunshot through the head from some jealous rival.

When they had successfully distributed five million fakes for a million new pounds, Ramsgate decided that enough was enough. After feeling a few chest twinges and noticing more grey hairs, he stashed his money in an offshore account and began hatching a plan to get out of the deal. The police were slowly closing in around the flood of counterfeit money that had turned up locally, and the bogus serial numbers were being recorded and advertised on warning posters in shop windows.

Everywhere he went, he felt the need to look over his shoulder. The game had got too dangerous to play. Frankie had his boys knocking off innocent people for no other reason than to feed his paranoia.

When a new batch of five-million fake pounds was ready for collection, Ramsgate envisioned a way out. Frankie ordered him to pick up the load and take it to Germany himself, and this unnerved him. Earlier on, in the yard, he had overheard a conversation between two of Frankie's henchmen; Frankie had found out about the second stash of twenties that had been circulating in the area, and he already had a good idea of where they had come from. If this was true and Frankie had Ramsgate pegged, then it was doubtful that he would survive the run. And even if he did, he knew it would only be a matter of time before he and Phil Jenkins could kiss their arses goodbye. If he was going to make a move, it would have to be now, before they made the move on him.

Ramsgate prepared himself emotionally by taking a few good deep breaths in. He hated these places and had felt that he looked guilty even before he had the chance to open his lying mouth. His palms sweat as he kept his head low, praying to God that he didn't bump into any of his contacts as he pushed through the heavy police station doors.

He felt like a demon about to take a sip of holy water and worried that he wouldn't be able to pull it off.

All he had to do was to appear as an innocent man, tempted by the fruit of the rich and not the callous criminal that he obviously was. There would be no going back from this. He had thought through every possibility that they could throw at him and had covered his back through the business. He planned to play the small fry and lay all the dealings at Frankie's door, explaining how he had lived in fear through the entire ordeal.

As he approached the Desk Sergeant he faltered and had trouble keeping eye contact. He was told to speak up as he weakly asked to see someone who had been dealing with the counterfeit case. At first, he told him to write down what he knew, and that he would pass it on to the relevant team. This made him anxious. He didn't want to be standing there in the public eye writing his fucking memoirs; he thought. His heartbeat was racing. He needed to talk to someone straight away. So convinced him that if he didn't, then a large sum of counterfeit money would soon be in circulation.

As he sat in the interview room, bouncing on his toes, he wondered if he had made an irreversible mistake.

He didn't want to be labelled as an informant as he had always hated them, but he didn't want to die either. Frankie would kill him without a second thought if he knew the truth, and this was the image he had to keep firmly in his head as he sat waiting for an inspector to arrive. He needed to erase all feelings of doubt. This was not grassing someone up. This was survival.

When the officers entered, he stood up, making it clear upon their entry that unless they could promise him some sort of deal, he would not be giving out any names or locations. He told them that this was too big an opportunity to pass up and assured them that the information he offered would put the whole of the counterfeit operation out of business.

Before sitting down, he pleaded again, insisting that they would have to look after him with some sort of anonymity. They seemed uninterested in his plight. It was only when he mentioned they might recover millions of fake pounds from distribution, as he knew where they were, that they eventually sat up and listened. They told him that if he cooperated, then there would be room for negotiation, but he had to give them more to go on before they could discuss exactly what would be on offer.

Originally, Ramsgate was going to admit to having a small involvement in the racket, if they offered him a deal straight away. But after a flustered start, he changed his mind and made the mistake of lying through his teeth about his involvement. Painting himself as innocent was the worst mistake he could have made. He told them he was just the manager of Hayden Haulage and had nothing to do with any fraud taking place. To his knowledge, the paper company 'Starling Prestige' was legit and just another customer using the company to transit their goods.

He had worked through the night tidying up all the loose ends of paperwork that may have linked him with the German company. By the time his desk was clear, he had convinced himself that by falling on the mercy of the police, he might just get away with it.

The fear was visibly real, and he didn't need to fake his appearance of it. He dug his nails hard into his hands as he relayed his story of him being the victim as best he could. He choked as he insisted; they were forcing him to drive the lorry with the counterfeit money aboard that weekend. He took sips of water with a shaking hand before blubbering out that if they wanted to seize the lorry and arrest Frankie, he would tell them where he would be.

Heather had been listening in on the interview from the other side of the glass. She had climbed her ladder through grit and hard work. As soon as Ramsgate said that he knew where the money was, she searched the police database to see if she could find anything about his integrity.

By the time she entered the interview room, she had enough on him to derail his innocence, but he wasn't to know, and she would keep it from him until bargain time.

'Hello, Mr Ramsgate. I hope my officers have been looking after you?' She smiled to put the man at ease. She knew that the more she played up to him, the more he would give.

'It seems to me that you have been in a very dangerous position for a long time, so let us try to see if we can help you back to safety.'

She quizzed him further about his work at the haulage yard and, by playing the good cop routine, had got him to tell her they had stashed the money inside the paper rolls. She had a good eye for a liar and pulled his story apart seam by seam without him noticing. His insistence of being an innocent pawn in Frankie's game was falling on deaf ears, as she already had him pegged, but it was fun to let him whimper on.

Her delve into his record had her wondering how an ex-criminal, convicted for fraud, had landed such a respected position with Hayden Haulage. She didn't have to wonder for long as, after speaking to the Hayden family, she got a faxed copy of his application form, giving her all the answers she needed. As she had suspected, there was no mention of his criminal record, and the referees were all fake. The statement from his last employer was interesting though, as it was from Frankie Thompson, a name she knew of only too well as a crook from her past. He had provided a reference stating that Ramsgate had worked as General Manager for him at

'Starling Prestige' for years. This was the link that Heather had been looking for. It blew his cover story of not knowing anything about the fake company right out of the water and gave her enough to charge him when needed.

When she told Ramsgate what she had learnt from his employers, he fell quiet. He wasn't expecting to be caught out so soon. The fluorescent light beaming off the four walls in the tiny interview room made his head spin. And after a few hours of persuasion, he admitted to the crimes. He saw no reason to name Phil Jenkins or the other drivers just yet and would keep them out of it until need be; he told the police that nobody except them knew about the hidden cargo.

After grilling Ramsgate for a further hour, they made a makeshift deal to apprehend the counterfeit money with him driving the lorry. Things were to go back to normal for now as not to alert Frankie. They put plans for the weekend drop off into place. Ramsgate could breathe again. He would soon be under police protection, and Frankie Thompson would no longer be an immediate threat.

* * *

The plan was for Ramsgate to pick up the full lorry from the loading bay and drive it to Germany himself. He had told the police the exact time that he would leave the haulage yard and they were to intercept before the lorry reaches the M4.

He tried to pull himself together and prepare for what lay ahead, but the fear was overwhelming. As he turned the key in the ignition, he hoped that this would not be his last journey and that he would soon be out from under Frankie's thumb, but he wasn't there yet.

His heart felt as if it would pump out of his shirt as he drove the lorry with the counterfeit money on board down to its drop off. He couldn't see Frankie's car or any of the other drivers that may have been around to help him unload, so reversed into position by the unloading dock. As soon as he turned off the engine, police cars swarmed at him from every angle.

Armed police were also in attendance and waited, squinting through their sights as the police ordered Ramsgate to get out of the cab. He came out slowly with his hands in the air, acting as an innocent man would. The police then seized him and slammed him down on a patrol car to handcuff him. He waited with his face pressed against the bonnet as they opened up the back of the lorry.

Everything looked legit, but he had informed them that the truth would lie in the paper's heart. They opened the rolls, one by one, and Ramsgate felt his legs buckle beneath him. He swallowed down the bile that had welled up behind his teeth and felt the blood drain from his face. For a second, he thought about running when they found nothing but the clean white paper in the back of the lorry, but knew that now there was nowhere left to run.

Frankie, it seemed, had slipped under the radar yet again and after checking out his address and his office, they deduced he had either had nothing to do with the counterfeiting or he must have had a tip-off from someone close to home. Apart from the fact that he had suspiciously packed up and left, there was no evidence that he had committed any crime to be held accounted for. Ramsgate, on the other hand, had spilt his guts out, so the police had to act accordingly. The familiar walls of Cardiff prison would soon welcome back a favourite inmate, but this time he would not say a word to anyone. He knew that one day Frankie would come looking for him and until then the dark would no longer be his friend.

Chapter Five

Three months had passed since the arrest of Ramsgate, and no one had heard a whisper from Frankie. Phil Jenkins had stopped looking over his shoulder and had warily climbed back into family life. He missed the extra money from his scam with Ramsgate, but not the stress that came with it. His anxiety had been off the scale of normal whilst worrying about the police knocking on his door. He would sweat in secret, keeping his morbid feelings away from Karen, his wife. He didn't want to worry her with his state of mind, as she had already lost one husband to suicide. He had figured that he would carry on around her as normal and leave her busy organising the running of the house and making sure everyone got to where they should be on time.

'Ruby, get your stuff together. You're going to be late for college.'

The raven-haired girl tutted at being pulled away from her phone. Her white face flushed with a hint of annoyance.

'Can't Phil take me? Ruby took a glance towards her step-dad, who kept his head firmly behind his paper.'

'No, Love he can't, he has to take Ben to school.'

Ruby raised her eyebrows then went back to her phone.

'I'll ring Jack then. He'll take me.'

Karen came in from the kitchen, her hair tied back in a loose bun and wet hands. She took the phone from Ruby.

'You're not disturbing your brother either—you know he works nights at that shitty factory. He doesn't get much sleep as it is with all that noise outside his flat.' She gave her the phone back after making her point. 'For once in your life, show some responsibility and get yourself to college.'

Ruby stood up, dried the phone on her jeans and screeched the legs of her chair. She threw her bag over her shoulder and buzzed around Karen.

'Can I borrow your car then, Mam? There won't be another bus for ages.' She looked over at Karen with pitiful eyes. 'Please—please.'

Karen wasn't up for the bickering so gave in and threw the keys to Ruby. 'Go on then and make sure you fill it up if you go off anywhere.'

Ruby left with a smile on her face and a half-eaten piece of toast in her hand.

It had been ten years since the death of Karen's first husband, Craig Lewis, and eight years since she married the love of her life, Phil Jenkins. As a long-distance lorry driver, he had spent a lot of his time on the road, and she missed his gentle banter when he was away.

They had an eight-year-old son, Ben, and although he was unplanned, he completed the family and kept Karen from spending too much time, wasting their money playing bingo. She felt they were becoming distant lately. She had spent little time with him, as he was always working. With the haulage yard returning to its normal legitimate business, she had thought that he would spend more time at home, but it hadn't been the case. This made her panic. A few weeks previously, she had found a letter in his pocket.

Phil, I know this is hard, but I can't control my feelings for you. It's driving me insane. I just want to be close to you. Please meet me.

It was scribbled on a piece of cardboard and had got damp in his high vis coat. The rest of it was unreadable, but this was enough for Karen to question him. Phil had told her it was one of the transport cafe girls. She had had a flat tyre, so he fixed it for her and now she wouldn't leave him alone. He said that she keeps leaving him messages when he goes to the cafe for breakfast, but he just puts them in his pocket then throws them in the bin later. He swore to her that nothing was going on.

He was a good-looking man and had a kind heart. Karen had met him in the local social club and had admired his blond wavy hair and golden skin. She had got herself into a state after a bad day and had been falling over drunk. He had seen her home and sobered her up. They talked for hours. She told him about the death of her late husband, and he had been a good listener. He had always treated her with respect. She didn't want to think badly of him, but he did seem secretive over his phone sometimes, and that unnerved her.

'Phil, do you have to go to Germany this weekend? Can't someone else do the run?'

He took his head from behind the paper and smiled at Karen. He loved his wife dearly and had felt the same about them not spending as much time together as they should.

'I'll see if Dave will take over. I can't promise you though, Babe, as you know what it's like with this new guy barking his orders at everyone.'

He rose to his feet, kissed Karen on the cheek and called up the stairs for Ben to hurry up.'

Ben, in his heavy Clarks' shoes, came thumping down the stairs at a snail's pace.

The beep of a text alert had Karen watching Phil from the kitchen as he took his phone out of his pocket to look at it, then quickly put it back in again. Ben pushed past his dad to get into the kitchen to pick up his lunch box, and the slamming of the front door finished Karen's morning routine.

Because of the school traffic, Phil was running late by over an hour. By the time he got to the haulage yard, Charlie Lane, his manager, was waiting for him to load his lorry and had a look of concern on his long-bearded face.

'Hey Jenkins, there was a girl here waiting for you, but she said she had to leave. She left you this.'

He gave him an envelope with a single red rose attached to it. Phil took the letter and apologised to his manager for the interruption to business. He was a stern man and not overly impressed with affairs of the heart.

'It's nothing to do with me, Mate. As long as you're doing your job, I don't give a fuck what you do. If it interferes with your work, then that's my business OK, now get on with loading. These rolls are for the German lot, and they don't take kindly to tardiness.'

Phil wanted to ask about him swapping the trip with Dave, as his run was only to the West Country. He hated Germany after the chances he took driving the lorries for Ramsgate. He looked at the new guy in charge and watched him pulling faces at the drivers who were standing around chatting, so he didn't think that now would be the best time for him to ask, so he put it out of his head.

Deep down, he knew he needed the money that the hours away in Germany would bring. He had lived beyond his means when they had the extra cash coming in from the 'dodgy money' as Karen called it. But now, the savings were few, and it left them with the aftermath of overdue bills to pay. He had told Karen to give up her job when they were sitting pretty and take a rest from standing on her feet all day in the supermarket. She hated him taking the chances and worried over every trip. He had been luckier than some, though, as a few of the other drivers that worked alongside Ramsgate had their marching orders. Phil had kept his job, as the late owner's daughter had a soft spot for him. With the police having nothing to link him to the counterfeit gang, he was happy to bow out and crawl under the radar.

He had paid off all his old debts with the cash he had made. But now, he had new ones that he struggled to keep on top of. They had tightened their belts and stopped the added luxuries they had become accustomed to, and Karen was looking to get her job back. His stepson, Jack, was not living at home anymore. This meant there was no extra cash to top up the weekly budget. Ruby was supposed to be getting a part-time job to help, but she hadn't even bothered to look. Karen treated her as if she was still a child and gave into her far too much for Phil's liking. She should pay her way the same as other twenty-one-year-olds, he thought.

He quickly opened the envelope and read its contents. It was much the same; a request to meet up. Phil put it straight in the bin with the rose still stuck to the envelope. There would be no chance of Karen finding that one. It would be bad enough breaking the news about Germany, he thought.

Phil loaded the rolls onto the lorry, secured the tarpaulin, then jumped into the cab to check the times and route. He went into the glove box and a pink cashmere scarf fell out onto the floor. He quickly pushed it back in so the boys in the yard wouldn't see it. They would rib him about it if they saw it, and he didn't need the hassle.

Out of the side window, he saw the manager checking off the loads with his annoying clipboard. The scarf had made him think about Karen, so he took it upon himself to ask for the rota swap.

'Hey Charlie, I don't want to give you hassle or anything, but is there any chance I could swap jobs with

Dave and do the one closer to home this weekend? It's the Mrs, she's been complaining of not seeing me enough—you know how it is.'

Charlie gave him a smug look and shook his head. 'If you weren't running around with other women, Mate, maybe your wife would get to see you more. I don't know, you drivers, you think you can come and go as you please. No—Phil, the answer is no. I need Dave to do another run for me this weekend as well. So, you're going to Germany, whether your wife likes it or not.'

Phil held his hands up and walked off. He had only been working with this new manager a few months and thought he'd be better off walking away before he opened his mouth and said something he would later regret. Now that those involved in the counterfeit money scam were no longer around Hayden Haulage was doing everything in its power to claw back the reputation it had when old man Hayden was alive. It was also obvious by the unmarked cars that were still hanging around that there was still a police presence watching over the firm's every move.

This new guy was running everything by the book. There would be no side-lines of dodgy dealings on his patch. Or so it seemed. He was ex-army and wouldn't stand for anything that resembled cross country double-dealing. Phil would have to come clean to Karen and explain that apart from really needing the money, Charlie Lane would not bend for anyone. He would have to wait for a quieter time to ask for the weekend off. Then make it up to Karen the way they always used to, with a bottle of wine and a night in a hotel somewhere.

'Shit!' Ruby muttered under her breath as she reversed the car onto the drive. She hadn't planned on her mother being stood in the doorway on her return. She watched in the mirror as her mother's expression changed to rage when she noticed the dent in her beloved Metro. Ruby had only been driving for six months and her mother was always dubious of lending her the car for that reason. To make things worse, she wound the window down and tried to make a joke of what had happened, explaining that she fought with a sign in college when, in reverse, the sign had won and had pulled off the number plate. Karen wasn't amused, and it showed. As she bent down to look underneath, she gasped at the extent of the damage, putting her hand over her mouth. Ruby rolled her eyes to acknowledge her mother's overreaction.

'It's only a little dent, Mam! Nothing to freak out about. The car's ten years old, anyway.'

Karen couldn't believe the audacity of the girl and screamed in her face.

'That's not the point, Ruby, and you well know it! And It won't be just me freaking out when your father sees it!'

Ruby got out and slammed the car door shut behind her.

'He's not my father—don't ever say that!'

She stormed into the house and up the stairs.

Karen stood staring at the dent for a while, then Jack turned up on his motorbike. He pulled in next to her and took off his helmet.

'Christ Mam, what did you hit?'

'Your bloody sister when she comes back down those stairs. She did this and thinks it's OK to take the piss as the car is over ten-years-old.'

Jack walked his bike to the side of the driveway and joined his mother in walking back into the house.

'Phil won't be very happy, 'he exclaimed.

Karen took one more look at her little car and shut the front door.

It was late when Phil eventually got home, and it was too dark for him to notice the car on the way in. He hesitantly sat down and told Karen that he would have to make the Germany trip tomorrow. Surprisingly for him, she was OK about it and he felt a woe lifted. Little did he know that her motherly instincts were now kicking in. And even though she was angry at Ruby, she didn't want her to have the wrath of Phil as well. This way she could get the car fixed without him knowing. It was an opportunity too good to miss.

The next morning, Karen put her plan into place. She got up early and moved the car to the next street down. Phil had not asked, but over coffee, she had offered the information to him anyway that Ruby had driven it to college again. Their time together was ticking away as he would leave that night for Germany and wouldn't be back until Monday or Tuesday. She hated lying to him but didn't want the rest of their Friday to be arguing over the car. She had more of an intimate morning in mind, so she made him breakfast and took him back to bed.

Their passion was interrupted several times by the ringing of a private number on Phil's phone. In the end, he turned it off and threw it at the wall. He told Karen that it would probably have been Charlie ringing and that he wasn't due in until later, so refused to answer it. He had an idea who it really was and had chosen not to answer it, especially in front of Karen.

As soon as Phil stepped out of the shower, Karen stepped in. He had already packed his clothes for the trip in a brown leather holdall at the side of the bed. After feeling around on the floor. He picked up his phone and put the battery back in. It had fallen out from hitting the wall. He sat on the edge of the bed in his towel, waiting for some digital life. When it powered up, he noticed he had received a string of text messages, and the last one sent him into a blind panic.

If you don't come to the bridge right now, I swear I am going to jump. I mean it, this is your last chance.

He quickly put his clothes on over his wet body and battled with them, sticking to his flesh. He apologised to Karen and told her it had been Charlie calling. Lying was the only option. He duped her by saying that there was some trouble with the load, and he would have to check everything before leaving for Germany. He smiled as he gave her one last kiss, then picked up his bag and left.

He weaved his way recklessly, speeding through the overgrown back lanes and across the field to the Oakland bridge. Adrenaline was seeping through his veins and he could feel his heart pumping through the muscle in his chest. All the worst scenarios were flashing in his mind as he struggled to keep control of the firm's car from skidding into the canal. He had tried to deal with the situation as calmly as he could. He could not be unfaithful to Karen and would not throw away his family. As he approached the bridge, Ruby was sitting precariously close to the edge.

He stepped out of the car into the mud and stood there, staring at the young girl he had known for the last eight years as his stepdaughter.

'So, you decided to come then.' She didn't look at him, just kept herself focused on the water below. He felt like rushing across to pull her away but knew that the reaction may cause her to lose balance.

'Ruby, please come down. I promise we will talk—just get off the wall.'

His feet were sinking in the mud, so he carefully guided himself around the car to the side path, wondering if he should get any closer.

'This was the only way Phil, you completely ignored me. I told you my feelings, and you just pushed me away. You don't understand how hard it was for me—to tell you how I felt.'

'Ruby, I love your mother. This would traumatise her if she knew. She already thinks I'm having an affair.'

He made a few small steps closer, and as she turned to face him, he could see the anger in her face. He smiled at her to bring her mood around.

'I love you as a daughter; the little girl that liked to watch Disney movies with me while chucking popcorn at each other. This would be wrong. Come down so we can talk…'

'But you kissed me.' Ruby interrupted, and Phil's idea of taking it slowly to get to her better side was wearing thin. He found the accusations ridiculous.

'It was a mistake. It meant nothing. I was drunk and half asleep. I thought you were your mother when you started kissing me in the chair.'

When he looked back at the situation, he felt Ruby had instigated the kiss all along and was now trying to turn it around on him.

'As soon as I knew it was you, I stopped, and if you're honest with yourself, you knew I thought it was your mother kissing me—didn't you?'

He was clutching at straws now and knew that he would have to use a tactic to make her see sense.

'How would Jack feel? He couldn't lose you. It would kill him.'

Ruby bowed her head as if to jump, then turned around at the last minute and eased herself down off the wall.

'Don't bring Jack into this. He's the only one — that has ever cared about me.'

'For Christ's sake, Ruby, we all care about you. Ben idolises his big sister. Think of what it would do to them if this family split up.'

He edged his way closer to her, not wanting to startle her into climbing the wall again.

'Look, Ruby, I'm leaving for Germany soon and I don't want this hanging over us when I return. Can we talk properly when I get back? I know you have feelings for me, but maybe you're just confusing them with the love you feel for me as a father figure.'

'I'm not confused Phil, you kissed me—fact.' She stormed off across the field, then turned around. 'Go to Germany, Phil. Go and make some money. I'll be waiting for you when you get back. Then we'll see what Mam thinks about it.'

Karen hadn't heard from Phil since he left. She had been trying his mobile, but it was going straight to voice mail. It was now Wednesday afternoon, and she was getting worried. She drove down to the haulage yard and met up with Charlie Lane.

'He delivered the load to Germany as scheduled and the lorry came back Tuesday. The keys were in the deposit box.' Charlie was getting aggravated that he was having to explain things to Phil's wife. 'That is all I can tell you. I asked around—nobody saw him—now I have to get on. If he turns up, I will tell him to ring you.'

Some of the drivers had drawn their conclusions, saying that he was still in Germany and may have arranged for the truck to be driven back by a courier. He had done that before, but that was when the merchandise inside had been too hot to handle. Others had listened to Charlie's story about the letter and the rose; making up their own sordid details about why he hadn't returned. Either way, no one was telling Karen what was going on and she worried about his safety.

Chapter Six

When they left the house, Heather insisted on driving to work. Gareth always seemed to drive in, and she hated the way he would stop at every red light. They were police officers, for Christ's sake. Surely, they were allowed to bend the rules from time to time. The new assignment needed her. Gareth smiled when he saw the tapping of her foot at the junction; willing the other cars to speed up so she could get to her desk.

'Don't get any ideas now that you're the same rank as me, Detective Inspector Williams. You're not driving in every day it makes you too tetchy.' Heather responded with a look that could melt ice. He tried to rein it back in, but Heather was not in the mood. 'Come on, Love, I'm only joking.'

'I know you're joking, but I get enough sarcasm at work. We may not be the most conventional couple, but you're my husband and should support me, not mock me.'

Heather had only recently got promoted to inspector, and she wanted to prove her worth to the chief inspector by turning up on time and getting her head straight into the job.

'It's taken me a lot of hard work to get here. I know that equality is moving out of the dark ages, but I still feel that some of the male officers think I shouldn't have had a promotion.'

Gareth put his hand on Heather's knee. He wanted to support her and knew that she was a much better copper than him. 'Don't be ridiculous Heather. You belong in CID. You're just as good as any male officer. It was your nose as a copper that sniffed out Bill Ramsgate. He would have got away with being labelled as a pawn in Frankie Thompson's racket if it wasn't for you. You had him pegged as one of the front men from the very beginning, and Sam Turner she would be dead now if you hadn't intervened.'

Sam Turner had been phoning the police, complaining about her ex-boyfriend Gavin Hunt for months. He had been stalking her at work and bumping into her accidentally on purpose. She lived two floors up, but would still check outside her window before going to bed. Too many times, she had seen him standing outside her block of flats, or sitting in his car, staying as late as four in the morning. She had tried to ignore it, but it was disrupting her life. She felt she couldn't even take the dog for a walk before work anymore as he would be there, in the dark shadows of the early morning park, in the guise of a jogger. Even though she knew him as a quiet man, and he hadn't attempted to speak to her, she still felt threatened by him. She stopped going out unless it was to and from work, and even then, she would look over her shoulder the whole time.

Each time he did something unusual, she would be down the station, begging for some support, only to be told that unless he actually approached her, then he had every right to be in the same places as her and there was nothing they could do. They suggested to her it may just be a coincidence, and that she shouldn't worry. One officer told her to just ride it out, stating that he would probably get bored and give up.

Heather had seen how the male officers had pushed aside her complaints. They would roll their eyes at her behind Sam's back as she repeatedly came into the station.

She decided that the woman had suffered enough and thought that it wouldn't hurt to take a PC with her and pay Gavin Hunt an unsuspected visit.

When she entered his flat, it smelt dirty. The furnishings were expensive and looked out of place amongst the piles of rubbish that were strewn around the floor. Take-away food cartons were congealing on the worktops and he looked as though he hadn't showered in months. As she went into the living room, photos of Sam Turner were staring back at her. They were plastering the walls held up by thick obtrusive masking tape. Most were recent photos. Heather had noticed that Sam had recently had her hair cut, so only a few were from when they were in a relationship. The most damning of the lot were the ones of her asleep in her own flat. Christ, he must have gained access somehow through the fire escape, and taken them, she thought.

When Heather questioned him about his memorabilia, he broke down in tears and confessed. When she ended the relationship, he became obsessed with stalking her and was planning on taking it to the next level. He admitted he wanted revenge and was planning on making her feel as bad as she had made him feel. He said that his life was over, and soon, so would hers. As he struggled to get out his words, he went to the kitchen drawer and pulled out a Bowie knife, at first Heather thought they had made a huge mistake not calling for any backup, but she gently talked him around and took control of the situation. After pouring his heart out, he admitted he had planned on using it that evening and fell to his knees. He handed over the knife and blamed his mental health, stating that he hadn't been the same since she finished their relationship. He had bought a ring and was planning on asking her to marry him. In a flood of remorse, he held out his hands and allowed Heather to handcuff him, then accepted his place in the back of the police car.

On the way in, he thanked Heather for listening to him. And told her he was genuinely sorry for all the trouble he had caused Sam. She could see that he was heartbroken and had been acting irrationally. Crimes of the heart were the worst ones to deal with, she thought. She had radioed ahead and when she got to the station, the mental health team was waiting for him. They would section him, and everybody would now be safe, thanks to Heather.

When they revealed their findings to Sam, she blamed the police for not taking her complaints seriously.

After learning she had been that close to death, she panicked. She wanted the police force to pay for what might have happened to her. Gently and with good intention, Heather talked her out of making an official complaint. She knew that if Sam went along with it, she probably wouldn't get anywhere anyway. It would be a long and drawn-out process, so Heather explained to Sam that she would be better off getting on with her life by putting it all behind her. She heeded her advice and felt forever in Heather's debt. Secretly, Heather would have loved to encourage the complaint to be made, but she knew it would only drive a wedge between the genders at the station, and things were difficult enough as it was.

Her old boss, Martha Moss, had reached the rank of detective superintendent. She had encouraged and nurtured all of her successes over the years. Heather had found her style of policing something to aspire to. They had cracked many a case together before she retired to her holiday home in Cardigan Bay.

Martha had a habit of acting on impulse. If she felt that losing time would make a difference, she would forget all about waiting for backup. This had been her downfall.

When she had acted on a tipoff that there was a dealer selling drugs to kids on the estate, she took chase on foot. The dealer's car cornered her. Before she could change direction, his accomplice shot her from behind.

Luckily, the bullet missed her vital organs. But had left her with limited use of her right leg. She could still walk but had to use a stick for anything longer than a ten-minute trek. Running after the bad guys was something she had to leave in the past. This had frustrated her so much that she retired from the force. She had always been the one in front and had felt too much of a burden to carry on.

When they were first married, Heather would visit her flat from time to time with her new husband. When they were alone, Martha would still question her why she had chosen him over her. She already knew the answer but persisted in asking.

When Martha was at the top of her game, she had no time for commitment, and Heather had felt a bit of a booty call. She would only want her around when the workload was easy, and this was hardly ever the case.

Heather wanted more, but Martha couldn't commit. In the end, friendship seemed a lot easier to handle.

DI Gareth Williams was still the only man that Heather had found a genuine connection with. She had found other men attractive, but none enough to break her special bond with Gareth. Their open relationship worked around her spending time with other women and him spending time with both sexes. They enjoyed the odd threesome thrown in for excitement, but always made sure there were no strings attached to other parties. They both worked hard and had no time for the chains of marriage, locking them into monogamy. Others had found their set-up quite bizarre, but it worked for them.

When they arrived at the station, the chief inspector was calling everyone into the incident room. Heather was glad that they had made it on time and knew that it had been the right decision to drive.

'Listen up people, there has been a body found at the cemetery.'

The whole of the office broke into laughter. The chief inspector shook his head.

'OK, calm down. This is not something to be laughed at. I don't know all the details yet, but a couple who were tending to their late mother's grave had noticed something hidden by the topsoil. When they reported it to the cemetery gardener, he took a look and found a body of a man buried on top of the new grave.'

Heather raised her hand. 'Do we have any idea who it is, Chief?'

'No, not yet DI Williams, we've only just got the call from the Duty Officer DI Brown.' The sniggers started up again, so the chief intervened once more.

'I will come down hard on anyone taking the piss out of where the body was found. So I want you horrible lot, on your best behaviour. Don't forget, this body has a name and probably relatives out there, so show some respect.'

The room returned to silence.

'I will be taking the role of Senior Investigating Officer. And because of her recent success with the counterfeit gang and the prevention of a possible murder, leading the case will be DI Williams.'

The office rumbled with disgruntled moans again, but this time for a different reason. The whispering and disapproving glares made it obvious that some were not too pleased with the chief's decision.

'Heather, in my office, please.'

The chief inspector sat in his chair and asked Heather to close the door behind her. His large bald head poked through the top of his hairline and the worry lines on his face carried years of exhaustive police work in its tracks.

'I chose you to lead this case for good reason. We need to have a bit of a shake up here at CID, too many officers living in the dark ages. I was talking to my old friend Martha Moss at the weekend, and she highly recommended your work ethic.'

Heather was pleased that she still felt so highly of her.

'So, let's see if you can step up to her expectations.' He shook Heather's hand before opening the door. 'All I ask is, if there are any big decisions to be made, you pass them by me first.'

She thanked the chief and joined the officers back in the incident room.

Heather wasn't sure whether she was ready for that much responsibility but would give it everything she had.

She felt as if he had thrown her into the deep end. The officers that were on her side were the best of the bunch; the rest she would have to prove herself to by keeping them in line.

She had been working towards this day since college. Changing her mindset to catch criminals instead of running from them was the best decision she had made from her younger days.

Her time as a young WPC on the Beechwood estate hardened her way of thinking. She had made a lot of petty arrests and some she lost sleep over. Even if the community there was tighter than a close-knit family, she had always feared that criminals may target her family for having a daughter in the force. Now, as an inspector, she would have to step up her game again. There was only one way to start a successful career, and that was to show them who's boss and allocate her team their duties.

She concentrated on issuing the right officers to the right jobs. Nurturing their strengths and supporting their weaknesses was the only way to set this up. Some of the old boys were stuck in their ways, swapping protocol for how they did it in the early days, so she wanted to keep them away from evidence hunting. She didn't want them deciding on the worth of a piece of evidence before she had had the chance to value it herself. They would be better on foot, she thought, surveying the surrounding house to house calls. An older copper would have more experience in sussing out suspicious activities and not be shy about acting on impulse if a situation didn't feel right. She chose the younger officers with their keen eyes as evidence hunters and sent them on the lookout for the unusual. Respecting any evidence found at this early stage would be crucial. She needed good documenting and for them to think outside of the circle of normality.

Working closely with her colleagues for all these years gave Heather inside knowledge about who would be the best people for certain jobs. She felt as though she wanted to do the entire investigation herself, but knew deep down that delegation was the best way to play it. She didn't want to burn herself out at the start in case she missed something vital.

When she arrived at the cemetery, she could see that Elijah Brown had done his job well as Duty Officer. Through the pathway of shadowing trees was the entrance to the resting places of the many. They had turned it into a circus with a wash of white tents against the dark grey headstones. The team had cordoned off places of interest and a PC was documenting access to the grave in question.

Heather looked around for Elijah. With everyone, including herself, dressed in white forensic suits, it was hard to make out which one he was. A catering truck had turned up through the gates and Elijah was reminding the driver of the sanctity of a graveyard. He told him to park outside away from any mourners, and watched it leave, followed by a swarm of officers wanting breakfast and hot coffee to wake them up for their early morning shift. He caught sight of Heather and shook her hand in greeting.

'Good morning, Inspector. Are you up to speed on what's been happening?' His strong Scottish accent stood out against the Welsh lingo.

'Not yet Elijah. I thought you might fill me in.'

'Nae problem. Shall we have a wee gander at the body?'

Elijah led the way through the tent, and Heather

was clocking the scene as she entered. The Divisional Surgeon had declared life extinct and now the police photographers were clicking over the body awaiting the SOCO's to do their job.

'Whoever put him there was a right chancer—who'd think of looking for a body in a graveyard? Aye, it's uncanny.'

Heather hated crime scenes. So many answers lay out in front of her, but without the knowledge of what questions to ask, they were still waiting to be found. Vulnerable to the elements.

'So, what do we know so far?'

Elijah scratched his head and grunted an answer whilst stretching his short but stocky body.

'To be honest, Ma'am, not a lot. The couple found him and alerted the cemetery. They sent for the local bobby and here we all are. None the wiser. As I said, it's really uncanny.'

'It sure is. Thanks, Elijah, I'll take it from here. You get back and file your reports. We'll talk soon.'

Mr and Mrs Cooper were sitting in the boot of their estate holding polystyrene coffee cups up to their pale white faces. It relieved them both to be interviewed finally, as all they wanted to do was go home and put the dreaded incident behind them. Heather had sent Gareth to take their statements. He had a calming manner and was good at drawing out the finer details.

'So, when you say, you noticed that the earth had moved, how was that exactly?'

The middle-aged couple looked at each other and both went to talk at the same time. Eventually, the woman was more forthcoming.

'We were putting flowers on Mum's grave. She only died a month ago, so the topsoil hadn't sunk in yet. We commented to each other that we were sure that we had left a wreath sitting on the top of the grave. We then noticed that someone had moved it to the grave opposite. That was when we noticed the hand.'

DI Gareth Williams had been scribbling away in his notepad and stopped dead in his tracks.

'Sorry, did you say a hand?'

The husband had found his voice and gave his version of the story.

'Yes, we noticed it when we went to put the wreath back on the grave. At first, we thought it was our poor mother, but you could clearly see that it was a man's hand. So, we went to report it to the gardeners.'

'Oh, my word, that must have been really distressing for you both. Sorry that you had to witness that, Mr and Mrs Cooper. We will make sure that your mother's grave is put back to your exact specifications.'

He gave the couple his contact card.

'Thank you so much for helping us. If you remember anything else or if there is anything we can do for you, just call us on this number. There is also the number of victim support if you need it.'

Gareth left the couple to catch their breath. He took PC Reid to one side.

'Poor buggers, imagine finding that. I don't think they knew what to expect. I'm confident that it's got nothing to do with them. Let's get a quick breakfast, then head back to the station. Heather wants me to go through the missing person reports.'

He watched the colour drain from PC Reid's youthful face.

'What's the matter with you? You're looking a bit grey, Mate.' He turned away and was sick around the back of the police car. He was a rookie and had never seen a dead body before. The thought of someone finding a hand sticking out of the dirt had turned his stomach.

Back at the station, Heather began decorating the incident room pinboard with locations. Hopefully, the blank spaces where the victim's name and other important leads would be filled soon.

Although the team was working around the clock, the information wasn't coming in as fast as Heather would've liked. They were strategically checking the CCTV cameras from outside the gates, but unfortunately, there weren't any inside the cemetery to catch any wrongdoing taking place. Not only did she not have a name, but no one could narrow down a time of death. The reason for him to be left at the cemetery was a mystery. Maybe the killer thought that this would be the last place someone would look for a dead body. There was no wallet or ID of any kind, and his fingerprints were not on file. This would be a hard one. She also knew that if there hadn't been a heavy downfall of rain washing the top layer of dirt away, he may never have been found so easily.

The only piece of information they had was a small bus ticket. It was hiding in the coin pocket of the jeans the corpse was wearing. On further investigation, they discovered it was for a German bus company. It caused a stir around the station and some officers were already making assumptions about it being related to the other corpses found connected to the counterfeit case. It wasn't much of a connection, Heather thought, but it was a place to begin the investigation.

While walking back to her desk, the chief stopped her in her tracks.

'I heard they found a connection to Germany, Heather. What are your thoughts on this being connected to the counterfeiters?'

'There could be a connection Sir—I'll send someone over to the depot. Do you have any new information on the suspects? Have they found the guys that created the printing plates?'

'No, Heather—it looks like they have gone to ground. They will show up eventually and when they do, we will be waiting for them.'

Chapter Seven

Karen's nerves were raw. Every time the phone rang, she would rush to pick it up, hoping that it was Phil. It had been three weeks, and they had shared not even a text between them. She battled with her sanity on whether to report him missing. Because of his involvement with the counterfeit gang, this could drop him in it from a big height if she interfered. If this was why he was keeping his head down, she would have to accept it, but the worry of no contact at all was eating away at her.

Ben had been asking where his father was every day. She told him and the rest of the family that he had been in touch, but his boss needed him to stay in Germany a while longer. They seemed to accept her stories and life was carrying on as normal.

The school run had been chaotic, as usual. The temporary traffic lights that the police had put in place by the cemetery were slowing everyone down. As she turned into her quiet little cul-de-sac, she saw a parked police car outside her house. At first, she felt like turning the car around, afraid of what was coming. But second thoughts had her worrying about her children, so she pulled on to the drive in anticipation instead.

As she got out of the car, Gareth met her with a sympathetic smile. She could see it written on his face that he was there to deliver bad news. As soon as PC Matt Reid saw Karen, he took off his hat and placed it tightly under his arm.

'Mrs Jenkins, is it OK if we come in? We have some news about your husband.'

Karen led them into the front room and Gareth told PC Reid to make her a cup of tea.

As they both sat down, Karen could feel every fibre of her body shaking. She had been in this position before and the still coldness of that time she would never forget.

'No—for God's sake please, not Phil.'

Gareth swallowed hard before nodding acceptingly,

'I'm sorry, Mrs Jenkins, but we have found a body matching your husband's dental records. We are not completely sure of the cause of death just yet, but we need you to come down to the station to identify him formally.'

Just for a second, there was total silence. Then, in a crescendo of grief, Karen wailed until every ounce of shock exhaled from her widowed body. It was more than any one person could endure in a lifetime. Both of her husbands dead, and she never had the chance to say goodbye to either of them.

Gareth let the woman have her time with her tears. He looked down at his shoes and patiently waited until she was ready to know more. Sadly, he had given this type of news a lot of times throughout his career, and each person's reaction was different.

PC Reid brought in the tea, but before he had the chance to ask if she took sugar, Karen interrupted him.

'How did it happen? Are you one hundred per cent sure that it's him?'

Gareth ushered the PC back into the kitchen with his hand. Then leaned forward.

'We are as sure as we can be at this time.' He paused for a moment with his fingers pressed gently across his lips, not wanting to bombard the woman. 'This may seem a little odd, but they found him in the cemetery.'

Karen was numb. Part of her was still waiting for him to walk through the door like she had been all the time he was missing.

'Mrs Jenkins—I'm so sorry to have to say this, but we need you to identify him for us—just to make sure, is that OK?'

She stood up and wiped the tears off her face with her sleeve before grabbing her keys. There was no point in putting it off. She had to know for sure that it was her Phil.

Heather was busy looking at the report sent over from the coroner's office. The body had virtually no sign of any apparent struggle, and they now knew that he was still alive when someone buried him. One arm had soil underneath it. And judging by the position it was in, it suggested Phil had raised it, attempting to climb out. This would have been an impossible feat with the amount of poison running through his system. The sheer weight of the topsoil would have been too much to lift in his condition.

After reading the statements that Gareth had put together regarding Karen, they made a positive link with

Phil and the company used by the counterfeiters. They already had a lot of the drivers banged to rights, but Phil's name had not been among the suspects. There was no cast-iron proof that he had taken part in any of the fraud, so too weak to build a case around.

On the way home in the police car, it suddenly hit Karen Jenkins that her beloved husband was dead. How was she going to tell the kids that Phil had died? Especially Ben. He was his dad, and he idolised him. She saw how hard it was for Ruby and Jack when they lost their dad. Ruby refused to talk to anyone except for Jack for months. They had always had a close relationship, and she had wished that they would let Ben in on their closeness, but they kept him at arm's length. This would be hard for Ben to face alone. She would need her oldest two to help him through his grieving.

Phil had made sure not to put any large cash injections into their bank accounts. Instead, they paid off their debts with cash. The police didn't need to know anything about that and she would not be offering the information. Phil's life was as clean as a whistle, and that was how Karen wanted him to be remembered. She knew he had been driving for the counterfeiters, and worried about the consequences. She wanted justice for her husband's death. But she didn't want his actions to have any rebound back to her family, so keeping quiet would be the only option.

At the funeral, Ruby had held Jack's hand for the entire time. Ben was too young to witness the burial but had attended the church. She wanted him to have good memories of his dad, not the image of a cold, hard coffin.

Her father had flown in from Scotland to support Karen. He could only stay for the funeral but had promised to be on the end of the phone if ever she needed him.

At the graveside, Ruby threw a single red rose on the coffin. Charlie Lane huffed. He commented to a colleague that he had wondered how Ruby had the cheek to be at the funeral next to his widow. Gareth overheard the comment. He had been standing behind him, acting as a respectful police presence. While the priest read the eulogy over the grave, Charlie kept shifting his weight from one foot to the other. He complained under his breath to one driver that the funeral was going on a bit. He moaned he was losing money and for them to get on with it. As soon as the main cars left, he jumped in his and Gareth followed him back to the yard.

Charlie Lane was sitting in his office when Gareth and PC Reid arrived. He had requested to be shown around the yard and in Phil's locker again. There was nothing inside apart from a spare jacket and some steel toe cap boots. They had already searched the truck, and that was the same. Apart from a woman's scarf in the glove compartment, the rest had been old sandwich boxes and empty pop bottles. Karen had identified the scarf as hers, although did not know how it got inside the cab.

'So Charlie, when the rose was thrown into the grave at the funeral, you commented. So what was that all about?'

Charlie raised his eyebrows. 'Well, she was his bit on the side, wasn't she? His wife was right next to her—now that's not right, is it?'

Gareth explained the girl was his daughter, Ruby. Charlie was not convinced at first and had explained about the time she had waited for him with the letter and the rose.

'All I'm saying is it looked as though she was waiting for him, like a girlfriend would, you know—I'm all confused now. I must have read it wrong.'

Gareth noted down the observations from Charlie and asked him to explain more about Phil's return from Germany. 'So, you are sure that you never saw Phil return the truck?'

'No, as I said before, sometimes they just park up and chuck the keys in the office. He hadn't signed out, though, which was quite unusual for him. I just put it down to tiredness. A lot of them like to sort out their paperwork the next day.'

'So, did you see him the next day?'

'No—the day he left for Germany was the last time I saw him. I feel a bit guilty really as he asked me if he could change his rota—he wanted to spend time with his wife, or so he said. I thought he was looking to go off with that girl—I do genuinely feel sorry for them now.'

All the leads Heather had regarding the counterfeit gang had come to a dead end. If there had been a price on his head, she couldn't find it. After they locked most of the gang up, there were plenty of squealers around exchanging petty offence clearance for information. She was sure that someone would have known about his murder, but nothing. Frankie Thompson had still avoided questioning, as no one knew where he was. They still hadn't found enough evidence of his involvement to go looking for him officially. Ramsgate was doing his time. And the chief was happy to let him take the blame for the entire racket.

They issued the full report on Phil's death the following week. Heather now had a diagnosis for death, poisoning. She had thought that she had been wasting her time pursuing a counterfeit gang connection. It was the chief that wanted her to stay with the lines of inquiry. But apart from the German bus ticket found in his pocket. And Hayden Haulage being his place of work. There had been no clues left behind on the body to suspect any foul play from a criminal gang. Poisoning and going to the trouble of burying a body was not their style, either. The victims that had turned up from the counterfeit gang had been shot, stabbed, or fished out from the bottom of the river. To make this series of events fit, she would have to stretch her investigation.

First, she would visit the family herself to see what type of people she was dealing with. She would keep it to herself for now as she didn't want the chief putting her off any leads for the glory of catching another fraudster. Second, she would ask Gareth to have another dig around at the haulage yard. Someone must have seen something.

When Heather pulled up to the house, Karen was standing in the doorway. As she approached, the acknowledgement hit her. Although she had aged over the last ten years, Heather recognised the woman immediately as the widow of the late Craig Lewis. She was only a PC at the time of his death and wet around the ears. She had never forgotten the way Martha had handled the inquiry. Working with her had taught her a lot about how to be discreet with information that would be better off unsaid and she always kept this in mind when interviewing suspects to this day.

At the time of the investigation into Lewis's death, they were looking for a reason as to why he may have killed himself. He seemed to have been content with his life and had no obvious stress or hardship to warrant a suicide. Martha had told her off the record that she had found out the reason, but wouldn't divulge to the rest of the force where she had got the information from.

She had concluded that Lewis had killed himself, as he couldn't live with the guilt of sexually abusing his daughter. So with this in mind, she had a moral dilemma to deal with and a tough decision to make. If she kept her opinion to herself, the girl would have a chance of growing up with a normal life. If the information were to be made public, the girl would have to suffer at the hands of an official investigation. There was no other option. She saved her from the intrusive medical examinations and kept quiet.

Heather remembered Martha's decision. She closed down a few of the lines of inquiry in haste without following the correct procedure. This was to avoid the ordeal from happening. This had surprised her. Martha wasn't the type to put her job on the line by perverting the course of justice. But when Martha reassured her that as he was dead, he would never pay for his actions, she understood. There was no need to expose the poor girl to any more suffering. Heather had thought at the time that Martha had known more than she was saying. So she respected her decisions without hesitation. She was adamant that she didn't want the girl being dragged through the courts and her intervention had made it so. The case was closed by Martha before it got off the ground.

Karen had never been told about the abuse. She thought the investigation had come to a natural end.

Heather, now in the position of an inspector herself, understood that the past repeating itself would be a devastating experience for the family.

'Why has this happened to me again? It's not fair. What have I ever done to deserve this?'

She cried hopelessly on Heather's shoulder. The recognition had been mutual and the feeling of losing her first husband mixed with her current grief overflowed her with emotion. Heather sat her down and tried to comfort her as best she could. When the tears finally dried, she asked if she could look around the house. She had learnt this from Martha as a way of getting to know the family in your head. This time, the place looked happy. There were no signs of any strained relationships and it was your typical semi-detached urban home.

'Have you any idea of who may have done this, Karen? Did Phil have any enemies? Or someone that he may have upset, or anything?'

Karen stared at her directly in the face. Everyone liked Phil. He had no enemies. There wasn't anyone apart from the counterfeiters that she could think of. She didn't want them to get away with it—if it was them, so she skirted the subject without giving too much away.

'Thinking about it. He had trouble at work a few months back. They wanted him to help with their dodgy dealings, but he refused. Do you think it's one of them? Would they have done this to him?'

Heather assured her that most of the counterfeit gang were now behind bars. She knew she had to divulge the details of the toxicology report but was now baffled by the similarities of the first husband's death. It wouldn't be easy, and she wondered how she would approach the subject. After all, everyone was a suspect in this case, as there were no obvious leads, she thought.

'Look, Karen, we now know how Phil died.' She watched intently for any reaction that may have given away an ounce of suspicion. 'He had poison in him. The same way as Craig. A high ingestion of Valium mixed with alcohol. Do you know anything about this?'

She flung back her head in despair. This was ridiculous, she thought. 'Why would he?—and how the hell could he? He couldn't have buried himself afterwards. Someone else must have been involved.'

'Karen—Karen,' she repeated herself as Karen had seemed to be completely out of the moment. ' I'm not saying he tried to kill himself, Karen, I'm just saying that the way he died was the same as Craig.'

As Karen sat staring into her coffee, Ruby returned home from college. She barely took the key out of the door before shouting out to her mother.

'What's going on? Why is there a police car parked outside?'

Finding her mother in tears as she entered the room, she dropped her bag and flung her arms around her to comfort her.

Heather pulled a chair out from under the table and ushered Ruby to sit down.

'Hi—Ruby isn't it? Your mother has had some bad news and needs your support right now.'

'Mam—Are you OK?'

'It's your dad, Love—they know what happened to him.'

Ruby pulled her closer and joined her in her weeping. Heather waited for the right moment before asking her if she could have a quick chat. The girl had changed so much in the ten years. She was a smart-looking woman, and Heather could see that she loved her mother.

'Ruby, I hate to do this to you now but I need some questions answered and I don't think that your mother is in any fit state to help us.'

'That's OK, I don't mind, anything to help. Do I know you? Your face looks a little familiar,'

It shocked Heather that it seemed her appearance had not matured with her mind.

'Yes, Ruby. I was the WPC that was helping with the death of your father Craig, alongside my colleague DI Martha Moss. You were only ten at the time. I'm surprised you remember.'

Heather followed her as she walked into the kitchen.

'How could I ever forget? It was the worst day of my life.' She paused and took out a bottle of wine from the fridge. 'I remember Martha. She spoke to me at the time and helped me come to terms with things. Is she still around now?'

Heather looked at Ruby and shook her head. 'No—just me, I'm afraid.'

She went to take two glasses out of the cabinet, but Heather declined.

'So, what happened to Phil?'

'That's what we are trying to find out, Ruby. It's a bit of a coincidence, but the coroner has said that his heart gave out because of the high levels of Valium and alcohol he had in his system—just like Craig.'

She took a long sip of her wine before reacting with a surprising comment.

'He was always popping Valium, so that doesn't surprise me. And he wasn't exactly Mother Teresa when it came to a bottle of whiskey either—so what happens next?'

Ruby held back on telling her what had happened between them. She had to tread carefully for the sake of her mother.

'Well, we do an investigation into who may have been the last to see him, then go backwards from there.'

'You do know that he was involved with some pretty nasty people at work, don't you? He was always shooting off to Germany at a moment's notice. Mam won't tell you this, but I'm sure he was involved with the counterfeit scam that was going on. That's where you should be looking.'

It surprised Heather that Ruby could be so candid. Karen had been adamant that Phil had nothing to do with any of it. The contradiction of character could be Karen not wanting to admit that he had flaws. She would want his memory to be pure, not like that of her first husband. She imagined that after he died, she would have spent a long time questioning why he would take his own life.

Chapter Eight

2000

'I've spoken to the family, Ma'am and they said that they just found him like that.'

'OK WPC Williams, just make sure that the kids stay upstairs. They don't need to see or hear any of this.'

Craig Lewis was known to the police for being a part-time robber, but not anymore. He was dead in his armchair. The Beechwood estate had lost another supplier of smuggled tobacco and bargains from the back of the lorry with no questions asked.

He wasn't a stranger to DI Martha Moss. She remembered him from the early days.

When he was younger, he used to work for her dad at the warehouse. He was always up to no good and liked to play practical jokes on the work experience kids. They would arrive expecting to gain experience of working life and leave feeling bullied and humiliated. He used to strip them down to their boxers and stretch wrap them to pallets. To make matters worse, he would forklift them to the top shelf and leave them there for hours, hanging in midair. Her father would never reprimand him for it, as he would condone much worse.

She remembered how he used to push Craig around. He pushed everyone around, including her. She hated him, and when he died last year, he died alone.

Martha didn't attend the funeral, much to the annoyance of her family. But then they didn't know of the years of abuse that she had suffered, and she wasn't about to tell them. If people knew, then she would be the victim and she couldn't cope with that. She couldn't change the past, so she used his death as her closure.

By the colour of Lewis's body, it looked as though he'd been there awhile. Five empty beer cans sat semi-crushed on the table next to the overflowing ashtray. She glanced around the room. There were no signs of a struggle; maybe he had simply died in his sleep?

The coroner's report would give the cause of death, but she still liked to put her detective skills into play. He was obviously a heavy drinker, but Martha had been more interested in the sediment she had found at the bottom of his pint glass. On a quick scan of the kitchen, she had found an empty box of Valium. Suicide maybe? she thought.

Heather came into the room. She looked at the family photos on the wall and felt sympathy for the little ones. The boy Jack was fifteen and the girl Ruby had only just turned ten. They had been asking her questions, and she had tried her best to avoid answering them. The wife Karen was in pieces and not making much sense. The only one who was asking the right questions and persisting for answers was Craig's brother, Rob.

'Any news, Ma'am?' it's just the family are asking?

'No—don't tell them anything yet. I'm thinking maybe suicide, but some things are not adding up. Who found the body?'

'It was his wife and brother, I believe.'

Rob Lewis had arrived to pick up Craig for work. After getting no joy from beeping his horn outside, he banged on the door. After a while, he looked through the window and noticed Craig sitting in the chair. He kept on banging but could see no movement. Eventually, he shouted through the letterbox, which woke Karen and the kids. Rob and Karen found him sitting there as if he were asleep. They checked to see if he was breathing, but it was too late. There were no signs of life.

'Did they move anything? Or find any clues to suggest that he may have taken something?'

'Not that I know of, Ma'am. They told me that when they realised he was dead, they shut the door, so the kids didn't see him, then rang us.'

'Can you ask Karen to come down and have a chat with us in the kitchen, Heather, and get Rob to stay with the kids?'

She nodded and left the room. Before climbing the stairs, she let the coroner's team in. By the time she had returned with Karen, they had their equipment all over the place and were treating the living room as a crime scene.

'Before we begin, may I offer you my deepest sympathy Karen, this is a terrible time for you and the children—I will be as brief as possible.' Martha put her hand on her shoulder. 'Is it OK if we call you Karen? Or would you prefer Mrs Lewis?'

Karen Lewis allowed the informality and sat at the kitchen table biting her nails. She smelled of stale alcohol and had traces of last night's makeup on her face, streaked by the heavy tears that had fallen that morning. She had gone to bingo the night before, and then for a few drinks with the girls. When she came home around midnight, Craig was asleep in the chair. They had argued before she left, and still felt annoyed at him for shouting at Ruby earlier.

'Can you remember the last time you spoke to Craig? It would help us piece things together.'

Karen stuttered her answer and sounded confused. 'It was about midnight—well, I didn't actually speak to him—he was in the chair asleep. I spoke to him before I left for bingo.' She pulled some kitchen towel off the roll and started wiping her face with it. 'I had a go at him for shouting at Ruby. She was so upset she didn't want to be left on her own with him. I told him to apologise to her.'

'Did they normally have a good relationship?'

'Yes, he's a good father. He always takes over for the bedtime routine, so I can get the house straight. Ruby just likes to push his buttons sometimes. Jack is always out, so she hardly ever sees him. I think she misses her big brother to play with. She hated it when Craig used to take him camping. She used to beg them to take her along, even when she was small.'

'Did he have any worries or problems that may have got on top of him…'

Karen interrupted. 'No—none. We were happy most of the time.'

'So, you—or Rob didn't find any note or…'

She felt uncomfortable with where the questions were heading.

'What! Why are you asking me this?'

'It's OK, Karen. That will do for now. Is there anywhere that you and the children could go while we finish up here? I could arrange for an officer to drop you off somewhere if you like?'

'We could go to my mams. I'll get Rob to take us.'

As soon as they left, Martha looked around the house. It was a typical council house; small and compact, with added damp. The inside doors were the cheap hollow core type. Someone had kicked them in at the bottom; always a sign of trouble, she thought. The master bedroom was basic and had piles of clothes on the floor. Jack's bedroom was a typical teenage hideaway, a dark space with a console and laptop.

Ruby's room was a little unusual. She had a lock on the inside of the door that showed signs of being forced open. She had drawn angry faces on her wall and had them hidden with pictures of Supergirl. Martha remembered her bedroom as a child. She had drawn on the walls as a cry for help, but nobody had seemed to notice them. This unnerved her a little.

When she got back to the station, she did a bit of digging on Craig Lewis. After hours of sifting, it quite surprised her that there wasn't much on him. He had a few juvenile crimes for stealing, and a couple of warnings for petty crimes, but that was nothing unusual for an estate kid. She noticed Heather was still at her desk and went over to give her mind a break.

'Fancy a drink, Heather? My shout.'

Heather didn't answer. She just stood up, put on her jacket and released her long blond hair over her shoulders. She didn't need to be asked twice.

The pub was quiet and a perfect hideout for two off duty coppers that were still sharing a flirtatious relationship. Martha brought the drinks to the table and smiled at Heather.

'So, do you want to talk shop? Or shall we talk about the weather instead?'

Heather felt that if she and Martha were ever going to get to know each other on a higher level, it wouldn't be from their conversation skills.

'We can talk shop—if you want to. I don't mind. I enjoy listening to your theories.'

She genuinely had feelings for Heather. But they were complicated due to her commitment issues. Her head was stronger than her heart. No one, not even someone as beautiful as Heather, would make her commit to anything other than a casual fling.

'Well, my theory is that WPC Heather Williams is regretting marrying that dork Gareth, so much that she would rather spend the night with me. Am I right?'

Heather laughed and nearly spat out her mouthful of wine.

'You've got some tickets on yourself, Detective Inspector. Why would I choose one night with you over the security and freedom I have with Gareth? I have never regretted marrying him. We live how we want as long as we are honest with each other.'

Martha screwed her face up. She couldn't understand how Heather and Gareth's arrangement had worked all this time.

'Face it, Heather. You love women. All this bisexual stuff is just…'

'Don't you dare say greedy! I fucking hate it when people say that.' Heather shook her head. 'You and me have spent plenty of nights together when Gareth's been on a night shift. But as soon as morning comes around, and we talk about general stuff, you get cold feet and clam up again. It's always just sex with you.'

She was almost right. Martha was used to looking out for herself, as no one else had ever bothered. She needed to keep her past and all that private stuff to herself. It had ruined her childhood, and she was damn sure it would not play any part in her future.

Martha had too many emotional scars on her brain. Her family was not the type to share problems. And never shared hugs. It was all about power and controlling situations to suit themselves. Martha was a mistake in their busy lives. Her mother was in her early forties and hadn't known she was pregnant until she was too far gone to do anything about it. Their son was all they had needed to carry on the family name. He had just left school and was away in college. They had finally got their house back to themselves, and then she came along.

The mental abuse began at an early age. Both parents were forever measuring her physical and academic strengths to her brother's achievements. She could not compete. He had been their golden child and no matter how hard she tried she could never outshine him.

The sexual abuse began when she started answering back. Her father would use her, then blame her for being born. He didn't need another female in his house. To him, they only served one purpose. When she was old enough to know what he was doing was wrong, she would scream. She would scream at the top of her lungs and throw things at him. He wasn't a big man and as soon as Martha had the strength in her body to hit back; she did.

That was the turning point for Martha. She left her toxic family home as soon as she was able and had pulled herself up ever since.

Martha moved in towards Heather and brushed the hair away from her face.

'And what do you think you're doing, Detective Inspector Moss?'

Heather always quivered at her touch.

'I'm hoping you will let me kiss you, WPC Williams.'

Heather rolled her eyes. 'Well, in that case, you have my permission.'

Martha's kiss was as warm and inviting as it had always been. But Heather knew where it would end up taking her, so politely backed away before she fell for her charm again.

'So do you have any thoughts about the case, Ma'am?'

Martha took the hint and stopped trying to seduce the girl. Talking shop would be the only connection they would have that evening.

When the news came in that it was a mix of Valium and beer that had killed Craig Lewis, the police were happy to rule the death as a suicide. Karen and the children were going to be left with no life insurance and a funeral to pay for. Rob was adamant that his brother would not have wanted that. He pleaded with the police to reopen the case and look at it as a murder inquiry. There were too many things that didn't add up. Rob told the police that Craig saw suicide as a cowardly way out. A real man should sort out his problems without putting stress on his family. He told them that their father had hung himself when Rob and Craig were still in primary school. This affected their relationships with everything. They both grew up with a traumatic loss in their lives. There was no way that Craig would have done that to his kids.

He had convinced Martha enough for her to do some house-to-house enquiries. The next-door neighbours' story was quite damning to the memory of Craig.

Joan Fisher accused him of being a monster. She said the little girl Ruby was always being shouted at by him and she had spent many an hour in her own house with her daughter Chloe, keeping out of his way.

The neighbour on the other side of the fence saw it differently. In her opinion, the little girl was always getting into trouble and her father was right to chastise her. She also accused Karen of not being squeaky clean. She had heard her chatting up her husband over the garden wall when she had drunk a few too many.

When asked, the rest of the neighbours shared mixed opinions about the couple. But all seemed to share the view that the boy was a little strange. He kept himself to himself and only socialised with his gang of emo friends from the estate. He was an excellent artist, but the artwork he had created was dark and disturbing. Jack was fifteen though and Martha knew from experience that busybodies always liked to voice opinions on hapless teenagers.

She was one herself back in the late seventies punk era. People were always calling her weird. She had swapped her studded jacket and black make-up for a subtler approach, but still found time to listen to the Sex Pistols on a Sunday morning.

Jack wore his black hoodie as a comfort blanket. He always hid his face and never had much to say. The only thing you could be sure of with Jack was how much he loved his little sister. They were as close as folded paper and when they were younger, inseparable. It was only now that he was a teenager that they had spent more time apart. Ruby hated it and begged him to spend time with her.

After going over the evidence and witness statements, she thought that Rob may have been right. There was no reason for Craig Lewis to have taken his own life. The crushed Valium at the bottom of the glass seemed an unusual find. Someone wanting to end it all would usually just swallow the bottle.

Martha made an unplanned, unofficial visit to the family home. It was on the off chance that they might shine more light on the suicide theory. Karen had just finished the dishes after tea, and Jack was about to head back up to his room. Martha asked him if she could have a quick chat before he left, and they both went into the garden.

'How are you coping, Jack? It must be hard being the man of the house and looking after these girls. Are you managing OK at school?'

'I haven't been back to school yet. I'd rather stay home and look after Ruby.'

'Yes, I bet she needs you right now. It must be hard for her to lose her daddy at such a young age. But you have to think of yourself sometimes.'

Jack stirred in his seat. 'I should have been here for her that night. She begged me not to go out as Mam was off to bingo—but I went.'

Martha looked intrigued 'Do you mean the night your dad died?' I'm sure it wouldn't have made any difference, Jack.'

'You don't understand, he was always shouting at her and…'

He shook his head, then got up to leave. Martha lifted her arm to stop him.

'And what Jack—Is there something else?'

He sat back down. 'I came home really late that night, and he was asleep in the chair. I opened the door to check on Ruby, the same as I always do. She had soaked the pillow right through by crying herself to sleep—again. There was an empty beer can in her room, so I knew he had been in there.'

Martha was feeling the children's pain. She went into Ruby's room and sat on the bed. She could feel something hard under the mattress and, after investigating, she pulled out a pretty pink diary with daisies on the front. As Martha turned to sit back down, Ruby came in and caught her with it.

'That is mine. Give it to me,' she screamed. She ripped the book out of her hands. 'You better not have opened it. Look on the front, it says private, see!' She had misspelt the word, but the sentiment was there.

'Sorry Ruby, I sat on it and wondered what it was. I haven't looked inside it honestly.'

Young Martha had kept a diary, too. She ended up burning hers, so no one would ever know what she had suffered as a child.

She reminded her a lot of herself at that age. Strong-willed but lost in a world of uncertainty. It was against protocol to talk to her without her mother present. But this may be the only chance to get to the truth, she thought. She would tread carefully with her questions not to overwhelm the ten-year-old.

'Ruby, is there anything in that book about the night that daddy died? If there is, you know that it's all over now, don't you?'

'No, I skipped that night as it was the worst.'

'Jack told me to forget all about it and promised me that if I didn't talk about it, or think about it, then it never happened, and I won't get any more bad dreams.'

Martha could see the logic that her brother had tried to instil in her and was glad to know that she had him looking after her. His way of dealing with things was like her own, so who was she to judge. If the diary contained what she assumed it contained, she would have the reason that Craig may have killed himself. She could put this episode to bed and concentrate on protecting Ruby. She would be the only thing that mattered. He was dead and couldn't hurt her anymore. The little girl had been through enough, and Martha would not let further interrogation take place.

'If you want me to take the diary, Ruby, I can make sure that nobody will ever read it, not even me. We can leave you and your family to get on with making better memories.'

The girl held on to it tightly with a frowned face and teary eyes.

'If I give it to you, do you promise you won't tell on me? I'm not a naughty girl, really.'

Martha could feel a lump climbing into her throat and she swallowed hard to keep it at bay.

'I promise. You're not a naughty girl, Sweetie. This will all be over soon, and you will grow up to be as strong as Supergirl. You have special powers like me and can be whoever you want to be. Trust me, I know.'

She handed the diary over and gave Martha an enormous hug.

'I already have special powers, I wished for Daddy to go away.'

Martha knew what she had to do. She didn't want that little girl handed over to the medical examiners. She had suffered enough. The diary would remain with her to avoid any further interrogation or upset to the child. If there was any need for a follow-up, she would say that they had misplaced it and would cover her tracks the best she could. She would keep Ruby's secrets, in the same place she kept hers, nestled inside a tormented brain.

Chapter Nine

2010

Ruby found Jacks motorbike in the factory car park and leaned against the shiny black metal, waiting anxiously for her brother. He saw her before she saw him.

He stopped, hitched up his backpack, and contemplated going back inside to avoid her. No point. She would eventually catch up with him anyway, he thought. He gave in. Making it obvious by his frustrated expression that he didn't want to see her, he dragged his tired torso towards her.

The night shift had been hard. He had got no sleep that day thinking about Phil. Halfway through, he had come close to fainting. After steadying himself, he made his way to the toilet.

Sitting there with his head on his lap. He blocked out the fluorescent stick lighting from boring into his brain. He was ready to drop. Walking back to his workstation, he could hardly keep his eyes open. The supervisor clocked it and gave him a warning. Ruby turning up and pushing her guilt onto him was all he needed. Each time she had a problem, she made sure that it became his as well. He had enough going on in his life without her adding to the stress.

The tale she had told him about her and Phil was constantly playing on his mind. Ruby, being Ruby, had purposely not mentioned that the attraction was only one-sided. She had kept out any part of it being instigated by her and had made it sound like a Jeremy Kyle love triangle. He didn't believe her at first, so she confirmed it by showing him the text messages that she had sent to Phil. Scrolling quickly past the negative replies from him, not wanting anything to do with her, she kept up the pretence of a relationship.

'For fuck's sake, Ruby, I don't need this shit straight from work. They have just given me a warning for falling asleep at the press. I could have lasered my fucking hand off—it's because of you. You're in my head constantly. Gnawing away at my brain.' He shoved her out of the way, got on to his bike and put on his helmet.

She stood in front of the bike with her legs on either side of the front tyre.

'I only came to say that the police spoke to mam yesterday about Phil. They told her he had died from an overdose.'

Jack pulled his bike back away from her and revved up the engine. He drove away at speed, leaving Ruby standing there. She wasn't sure whether he had heard her, but at least she had told him, she thought.

As Jack drove the long journey home, he could feel his eyes closing at every turn. He shook his head and opened his visor to get some air to his face. As he waited at the traffic lights, he must have only fallen asleep for a few seconds, but the car behind him hadn't noticed. As the lights turned red, Jack stayed still, and the car bumped him from behind. He fell sideways, hitting his head with the weight of his bike on top of him.

The driver got out and started panicking while onlookers phoned the police. The man who was in his late sixties was beside himself with worry, as he had never had so much as a parking ticket before, let alone an accident of this type.

The ambulance siren woke Jack's unconscious state. After pulling himself out from under his bike, he tried to stand. His legs buckled from underneath him so the lady that had been helping the distraught driver steadied him back on the ground.

The ambulance staff asked him question after question. But all he wanted to do was get home. He was refusing to go to the hospital and was trying to assure the paramedics that he was feeling fine. They sat him in the back of the ambulance and checked him over. When they found out that he had lost consciousness previously, and was still very unsteady, they convinced him to let them do their job and take him in.

* * *

When Ruby arrived home, the house seemed still. Her mother was sitting in the kitchen, hugging a cup of coffee, and staring into space. She didn't want to disturb her in her grief, so headed straight upstairs.

She could hear whimpering coming from Ben's room, so opened the door ajar to see what was going on.

She found him sitting on his bed, taking apart his wrestling figures and boxing them up. He had attempted to play with them but gave up, throwing them into the box.

‘Hey Ben, I thought you loved these. Why are you putting them away?’

The boy hugged the box to himself and gave her a look to melt ice.

‘These are mine — Dad gave them to me.’ He let go of the box and knocked it to the floor. ‘I don’t feel like looking at them anymore. They remind me too much that—he’s not coming home.’

Ruby put her arm around him and, through his tears, helped him dismantle the rest.

‘I miss him, Ruby. I don’t even know what happened. Mam was on the phone earlier with Grandad and she said that he had taken some tablets. But tablets are supposed to make you feel better, aren’t they?’

Karen had been talking to her dad and trying to make sense of it all. They had been comparing the deaths of her two husbands and Ben had got confused with only hearing the one side of the telephone conversation.

‘He loved you very much, Ben, and that is all you need to know.’ She brushed his hair out of his sodden eyes and gave him a big sisterly hug. 'Come down and I'll get us some ice cream, yeah, the one you like.'

A phone call from the hospital interrupted them. The news of Jack's accident had reached Karen. She was distraught and immediately let out the tears she had been harbouring that afternoon. They told her not to worry as he had only suffered superficial wounds. Losing consciousness, though, was always a cause for concern, so they were keeping him in for the night just for observation.

Even though the hospital staff had insisted that he was OK, she still rang a taxi to take her straight down there. With all the trouble going on, she still hadn't got the car fixed properly after Ruby bashed it and she wasn't in the mood to be kneeling on the wet ground sticking the number plate back on with sticky tape.

When she arrived the doctor said that his obs were stable and Jack would be back on his feet in no time. There were no major injuries, but he would have to take it easy with the concussion.

When he awoke from his nap, it shocked him to see his mother's face. He had been dreaming that she had died, so reached out and held on to her tightly.

'Don't leave me Mam—promise me, no matter what, you will never turn your back on me.'

Karen had put his strange sentiments down to being delirious. She loved her boy and knew that even though he was a loner; he cared about his family and had always wanted to be a closer part of it. He had a good heart but had spent too much time inside his head worrying about things. She decided that on his release, she would take him home with her. She would look after him. Keep her family safe. It would also be good for Ben to have his big brother around with him, losing his dad so suddenly.

Although Jack was fifteen when he lost his father, Karen remembered how he would clam up and not want his name mentioned in the house. He got into trouble at school and was hanging around with a different crowd than his usual steady lot. He had always been the type of boy that was picked on but had turned into a bully himself. His old friends, of which there were few, had become his hunting ground and the weaker ones suffered.

Josh had been Jack's friend since primary school. They had spent a lot of time together watching sci-fi films and going to Star Trek conventions. After his dad's death, he didn't care about past friendships, he just wanted to drink himself into oblivion every night with the kids from the far end of the estate.

They were sitting on top of the garages and had spotted Josh coming out of his house with his new creation of the Star Wars Death star in Lego. He was on his way to the sci-fi club to show off his masterpiece when Jack and the boys sneaked down the side and jumped out at him. Josh dropped his creation and looked at Jack to take his side. Instead, Jack stood on the creation and left it in a thousand Lego bricks.

The boys laughed and walked away. When Jack heard Josh weep, he went back. He pushed him to the floor and pummelled the boy with his fists before kicking him hard to the body and head. It was that violent that the other boy's laughter turned to fear, and they ran off and left him to it. Then he stopped as suddenly as he had begun. He pulled his hoody up over his head and walked away.

No one chastised him for the beating, as no one had the guts to grass him up. After that night, he stayed away from everyone. It changed him. He couldn't condone his actions. Why would he react like that with no reason or warning? His temper was something to keep locked away. The only one he told was Ruby. On hearing the story, she didn't flinch from her cold, white expression. Whatever her brother did would make no difference to the amount of love she had for him. He was her protector, her hero.

Ruby had stayed home to look after Ben. She wanted to go but wasn't sure whether Jack would have wanted her there, anyway. He would probably blame her for causing the accident, even though she was nowhere near him. Their relationship had always been strong, but since she told him about her involvement with Phil, he had not taken too kindly to the news. He had tried so hard to avoid her and stay clear of her drama, but she wouldn't let him. She would always want them to be a team in whatever was going on. And she wouldn't let him forget it.

Chapter Ten

When Heather got back to the office, she found out, to her annoyance, that Gareth had left a lot of the surveillance of the CCTV to the rookie. They wasted all that time. Not that he would do an awful job, it was just a more experienced officer would notice the unexpected.

After sending him out to get her a coffee and some lunch, she rearranged her plans for the day. She would sit in front of that screen until something jumped out at her.

Streams of grieving family members were paying their respects to loved ones. These were mainly on foot, leaving their cars in the pub car park opposite. She took special care when watching the hearses drive in, though the black attire made everything harder to distinguish.

There had only been two other cars passing through the gates so far, and both were carrying mourners.

After her third coffee and second sticky bun, something in the background caught her eye. She rewound the tape several times and slowed down the footage. It was a small dark car passing back through the gates at the same time as the funeral cars had entered. The size of the black Daimler limousines had shielded it for most of the way, but you could clearly see it for a split second when it left.

She would get the experts to work on the image and enlarge it. Hopefully, an image of the driver may be enhanced, or a number plate would be part visual.

She went back through the early footage but couldn't see when the car had entered. If it had come in through the other side of the cemetery, they would have no chance of tracking it. Unfortunately, the camera on that gate hadn't worked in years.

The nearest traffic camera was half a mile away. She instructed PC Reid and a few of the others to go through the footage from it and look for a small, dark car. Twelve hours on either side of the time of the cemetery footage would be enough. It would be a mighty task, but this was all she had to go on for now. If it was just another mourner, at least she could rule them out of her enquiries.

The family had no more information to give. It would be up to Heather and her team to find the answers. The coincidence of the death of the two late husbands of

Karen was still very much a concern. Surely, a coincidence as tight as this was unusual.

She could remember most of what had happened, but as she was only a WPC, she wasn't heavily involved in the case. She needed to go through everything from ten years ago to refresh her memory of the death of Craig Lewis.

The computer database was sparse. Martha was never one for technology and had insisted on doing a lot of her filing on paper. She dug out the case file of his death and it surprised her at just how little information there was.

Normally on deaths like his, there would be boxes of statements and scene of crime reports, but the file was noticeably thin. This would be down to Martha's involvement, she thought. There were a lot of unfinished headed files with no paper trail to follow, and they had tagged nothing for the evidence room. The bulk of the reports had come from the brother Rob Lewis demanding to have the case reopened. The statements were pretty grim reading.

There is something not right with that girl. The reason he was always shouting at her was because she was always naughty. She killed his pet snake, did you know that? She stabbed him with pencils—he found it in the cage one morning with her fucking Barbie pencils stuck in its back. She was evil.- Rob Lewis 2000.

She played with my daughter Chloe. She used to take her toys and refuse to give them back. She was cruel sometimes, but I blame the father. He was always shouting at her. My bastard old-man is the same. I was glad when they put him away. They like to rule over the little ones. I wish he would take some pills inside, put us all out of our misery.- Joan Fisher 2000.

There was no way he would kill himself. There must be more to this. He wouldn't have done it to his kids. They had their problems but nothing to kill himself over. I feel sorry for Jack. Everyone thinks he's weird. He's just a quiet boy, not like his sister. She would scream blue murder if she didn't get her way. Not even Craig could keep her under control - Rob Lewis 2000.

After sifting through the statements, she was unsure of whether Rob Lewis may have had a point. If he wasn't abusing her and just chastising her from time to time, maybe there was no reason for him to kill himself. She would ring Martha and maybe pay the old bird a visit.

* * *

Heather had not yet had the pleasure of visiting Martha's new house. It was in the middle of nowhere and Heather had argued with her satnav the whole way. It had taken her up dead-end lanes and across mud-paths for the last two hours. When she eventually found it, Martha was out in the garden feeding the goat.

Heather couldn't believe how life had changed for her old boss. Jeans and hiking boots had replaced the smart suits and shiny shoes. She still found her sexy, though in a rugged sort of way.

The sea air had given the outside of the house a battering, but it had held its own against any storm that would have made the waves lick at it from below. It was quaint rather than small. But big enough for Martha and the 'Muffins' as she liked to call them. Her faithful Labradors, Lola, and Moose.

She also had a friend with benefits that would come over to stay from time to time, so she was never lonely.

After being introduced to the dogs by them jumping all over Heather's smart two-piece, the old friends sat with a steaming pot of tea and a half bottle of whiskey.

'So my girl, you're an inspector running your own case now—I knew you would climb the ladder. You always had a good nose for a suspect. I'm proud of you.' She poured the whiskey into two small glasses and necked a quick one before refilling, 'So, what was so urgent that you couldn't explain on the phone?'

Heather knocked her glass back too and grimaced at the taste. 'Do you remember Craig Lewis? They found him at home in his chair after committing suicide.'

She picked up her cane and went over to her Welsh Dresser. She'd filled it with case files and old bits of memorabilia from her time with the force. Reaching up to the top shelf, she pulled out a folder that had a few loose papers in it.

‘Yes. I remember him? She showed her a copy of a photo that had been hanging on the wall at the house. Nasty piece of work, he used to work for my father—he did the world a favour when he topped himself.’

‘I remember you thought that the reason he had topped himself was that he had abused his daughter. Did you find any proof of that or…’

Martha interrupted her, ‘Proof—you didn’t need proof. You could tell by the way his daughter acted; she had been through hell at his expense. The poor thing was terrified. If I hadn’t stepped in, they would have had the medical examiners all over her. She was only ten and had been through enough. The best thing for her was to forget it ever happened. He was dead—he couldn’t hurt her anymore.’

It surprised Heather, the way Martha had reacted. She wondered then if she had ever experienced anything of a similar sort, but was too afraid to ask.

‘There was a pink diary that the girl had written in. She had drawn pictures, too. I only stomached it for a few seconds then put it in a box file. It’s here somewhere.’ She started pulling out drawers and moving things around. 'What's this all about, anyway?'

Heather didn't know if it would be relevant, but they were no closer to finding out how Phil died, so thought that it may flag something up.

She explained to her about the Valium found in Karen's second husband's body. And the unusual place where they found him. It amazed Martha that there had been no CCTV footage of value from inside the cemetery.

'Did you check the hearses that were coming and going? Was there anything different about any of the drivers? They had to have got the body in their somehow kid. Maybe you're just not looking hard enough.'

Heather was feeling a little overpowered by Martha's questions. Gareth had made the wrong decision not going over that CCTV footage himself. She hoped that by now, they may have enhanced the image and traced the car and driver. She didn't mention it to Martha just in case it turned out to be a mourner.

'So how is the girl? Ruby wasn't it? Did she grow up living a normal life? Or did that bastard's memory taint her?'

'Yes, she seems fine. Hard around the edges, but her mother says that she is doing well. She's in Oakdale college doing law studies. They seem to have all turned their lives around since leaving the estate. You were probably right about keeping her secrets for her.'

Martha smiled. It had been a hard decision to make. One that had kept her awake at night. She was glad to hear that it had been the right one. Heather continued.

'The boy is still a bit of a mess, by all accounts. He has been known to us over the years for possessing cannabis, but his mother doesn't know this. He's twenty-five a grown-man it has nothing to do with us what he tells his mother.'

'Well, you can't blame the boy for smoking a bit of weed. We did it enough, hey Heather. All those nights in the Feathers. At least we were off duty and not on the heavy stuff. Not like now, with all this cocaine being brought in. Every time I go to the station to catch up, there seems to be someone there off their tits.'

'It's the pressure of the job and the freedom of suppliers these days. Gareth said that they were all on it when he was working in Vice.'

'Gareth, argh, the lovely Gareth. You would have ended up here with me if that pretty boy hadn't turned your head. So, are you two still together? Or has he left you for some nubile PC?

Heather laughed. Martha had always hated the fact that Heather batted for both teams. But deep down Heather knew that Gareth was the only man that had turned her head. The rest of her acquaintances had been women. Gareth would have his head turned by either, and that was why their marriage worked.

'So, I would have ended up with you then, you think? You, me, the dogs and the goat.'

Martha laughed. 'There's nothing wrong with that goat. He'll eat anything.'

'A bit like you then, Martha.' Heather scoffed.

Martha got closer to Heather and kissed her cheek. So, do you want to see upstairs, just for old time's sake?'

The question did not surprise Heather. Martha still had that look of wanting in her eyes that could convince her to do anything.

'We had something—didn't we? Can you remember how good we were together?'

Heather remembered. Every touch from Martha had taken her to the brink of heightened palpitations. She remembered how soft her lips had tasted and that no one had ever claimed her body in that way.

With the sound of the sea crashing against the rocks, she had the feeling of an old black and white love story floating around in her head. She didn't want Martha to see her need for her just yet. Martha had made her wait for her many times in the past, and it had made her feel dismissive. This time she wanted to be the one in control, but when Martha kissed her again, she felt her knees buckle. All claims of power slipped away from her as quickly as they had in the past.

The large open windows gave no fear of privacy as Heather slowly undressed for Martha. Each movement had given Martha an ache of passion that so desperately needed fulfilling. Heather climbed on top and straddled Martha's body. A small gentle kiss followed each release of a shirt button as she made her way to her neckline. Martha's body lifted as she flicked open the button on her Levi's and slowly slid her hand inside. She could feel her swelling under her fingertips as she entered her, again and again, each time with more intent, each time a little deeper.

Martha rolled Heather to the side of her and held on tight around her neck. Under her pale palms, she could feel Heather's nipple harden, begging to be warmed by her mouth. The circling of her tongue made Heather more aroused and with each movement, she breathed a deep sigh of pleasure, forcing her to be claimed by Martha. As Martha trailed her hand to the top of her leg, Heather sighed. She entered her. It was a touch that she had remembered well. The more she manoeuvred her fingers around, the harder it was for Heather to hold back from her climax. She had lost all feeling in both of her legs, and this made it unbearable for her not to lose complete control. Lifting her hips one last time, she groaned deeply, begging her to release the pressure she had created. As they reached their climax together, they held on to each other tightly. Not wanting to lose the familiar feeling of their togetherness.

The next morning, Martha woke up alone. The same as she always did. This time she had broken her code of not wanting anything more and had asked Heather to stay the night. She had declined. Martha now knew that the time of Heather wanting a relationship with her was truly past. This had made her want her even more. She had never chased the girl as she had always been there, hanging on her every word. But the time apart these last two years had made Martha realise Heather was the only one that she would ever consider having a relationship with. Hers was the only photo that she had kept, safely hidden away at the back of the drawer.

She had a quick shower, dressed, then went to the drawer to find it. Going through the old stuff brought back so many memories of the time they used to work together. Especially, the death of Craig Lewis. The news of Karen losing a second husband had her intrigued, so she looked for the diary she had taken from Ruby.

When Martha's father passed away, it left her with scars that could never heal. She could never forget what had happened to her when she was a child. But had come to terms with it more now that her father was dead and buried.

She had locked away the book for Ruby, as promised. There had never been a need to see its contents, as she could sadly imagine what secrets it would reveal.

The book fell open on the page she had remembered. The hand-drawn pictures were graphic. She quickly flicked past, not wanting them to leave any impression on her mind. The cries for help were there, written in black and white for all to see. There were more drawings further on that turned her stomach, but then she noticed a page with different handwriting from the rest. Its contents alarmed her.

No more sad Ruby. Daddy is asleep forever. He drank his medicine like a good boy and closed his eyes. Bye Bye Daddy xxx

Martha was not aware at the time that the child had seen or heard anything to do with her father's death. This had put her in a difficult situation. If she took the book to the station, they would know that she had withheld evidence and she would be in a lot of trouble. But if she kept quiet, who knows what might have happened in the mind of a troubled child?

The words, in different handwriting, unnerved her. It caused her to build her scenarios in her confused head.

Had someone else poisoned the man, and she had witnessed it? Or had she written in different handwriting with a fractured mind? She had heard of this before and seen cases where a child's personality had split through abuse. The child would then take on a new personality to block out the past.

She wasn't sure whether she should tell Heather, as she didn't want her involved with the cover-up of the first death.

Heather had told her that Ruby was studying law at Oakdale college. She knew it would be totally unethical, but decided she would visit her. She would only have a ten-year-old Ruby's face to go on. And hadn't a clue what she would look like now. But she had her name. She would use her old police ID to flash at the receptionist and find the girl.

The intern escorted Martha to the room where Ruby was studying. She pointed out to her which one was Ruby, so she waited until the class had finished before confronting her.

She sat in her car at the exit of the college, waiting patiently for the girl to leave. She had not yet worked out how she would approach the subject but knew that this would be the only way she would get any answers off the record.

Streams of students passed busily on their way out. At first, she panicked, thinking she had missed the girl. Then, as she was about to leave, she saw her and walked hesitantly towards her.

‘Hi, Ruby isn’t it? Look, sorry to disturb you—do you remember me?’

The girl didn’t at first. It unnerved her that a stranger was asking questions in a student car park. After Martha showed her police ID, she walked with the girl and they sat under the shelter in the waiting area.

‘I know it’s been a long time Ruby—and you were only little then…’

Ruby interrupted. ‘I know who you are. It’s Martha, right?’

After speaking to Heather previously, it was easy to place Martha’s face into the faded memory she had of her from the past. Martha was pleased that she had a recollection of her. It would be hard enough bringing up the past as it was, but if the girl had some kind of memory of her, it would make things a little easier.’

'You came to help after my dad's suicide. I remember you telling me that everything would be OK—and it was. Are you here because of Phil? It's terrible what has happened but I don't have a lot of time to chat, I really have to be somewhere.'

Martha gave Ruby her card with her number and home address.

'Listen, Ruby, I really need to talk to you when you have the time.'

'OK, but not now yeah, I really do have to go.'

As the girl attempted to leave, Martha continued.

'Do you remember Ruby—that you held a lot of bad feelings towards your father before he died?'

Ruby was silent for a few seconds and just stared at Martha.

'It was childhood stuff. He wouldn't let me go to Chloe's and I was angry at him—I can't remember anything else, sorry. Look, I do have to go. Jack is coming home from the hospital today. Is there something I can help you with? Or are you really just here for a catch-up?'

Martha smiled, but behind the gesture, she knew that this would be her only chance to get to the truth. With each remark that Ruby made, she felt it slipping away.

'Are you sure you can't remember anything else?

Ruby was getting frustrated and pulled her bag up on her shoulder to leave.

'For Christ's sake, woman, it was over ten years ago. It was a terrible time for me, to be honest, I don't want to remember anything.'

Ruby's harshness took Martha by surprise.

'You gave me a diary—and yesterday I saw it mentioned about your father's suicide…'

Ruby interrupted abruptly. 'Wait, wait, you haven't still got it, have you? You promised me you were going to throw it away. It was private.'

'So you do remember some things then? Sorry Ruby, but I promised you I wouldn't read it and until yesterday I hadn't. It's been sitting at my home in Cardigan Bay gathering dust.' She watched as the girl's facial expressions showed contempt. 'You were a frightened little girl back then and didn't have the words to give me an explanation.'

As Ruby listened with a hint of confusion, Martha could see the girl from ten years ago staring back at her.

She had the same lost look of a child, but now on the face of a woman.

'You wrote about what happened to your dad. You wouldn't have been able to write that unless you saw something or knew something about it.'

Ruby stamped her feet on the floor and turned with a scowl to Martha.

'Look, you took that book from me and spoke to me without my mother being there. And as I was never questioned again, I presume you kept a lot of the details about what happened from the police investigation.' She pointed at Martha, and the retired police officer felt a bit intimidated. 'You need to leave this alone because if this gets out, you will probably be in a shitload of trouble.' She got up, walked a few steps, then turned back again to Martha. 'The past should stay dead, Martha. Stop the questions, OK.'

Ruby was right. There would be a lot of fallout from her not following the correct procedures in the past. She had to keep trying, though. Something didn't feel right. And Ruby was the only one with the answers.

'Ruby, we need to talk about this. I can't just forget what I read.'

As Ruby walked off, she flipped her the finger and Martha saw a different side to the sweet little girl from before. She would have to come clean to Heather. It was the only way.

Before Martha returned to home to Cardigan Bay, she went back to the Beechwood estate to take a look around and ignite her mind with memories of the past. There were many changes to how she remembered it. The council had re-painted the houses and tidied up the communal areas, making them more pleasing to the eye. It still had the look of a council estate, though, with its brand new graffiti from the Beechwood Posse adorning the walls.

When Martha was there last, it had been to visit a boy who had suffered a beating on his way to a sci-fi club. Little did she know that this, too, was connected to Ruby through Jack. She remembered how scared he had been and that no matter how hard they pushed, he wouldn't give out the name of who committed the crime.

Chapter Eleven

When Ruby got home, she was pleased to see that her brother was on the mend. The cuts and bruises were healing nicely and, apart from a few dull headaches, he was back to his old self. The feeling of gladness wasn't mutual, and by the scowl on his face, he wasn't pleased to see her.

'I wouldn't be in this position if it wasn't for you. You're so self-absorbed and always in my head.'

Ruby had thought of having a go back at him but knew what he was saying was the truth. She always confided in him and turned to him in times of trouble. Martha digging up the past was the last thing she needed right now. There would be a lot of questions to face. She couldn't do this alone. Jack would have to be her saviour yet again.

'Look, Jack, I know that I'm a handful most of the time and I do honestly regret dragging you into things, but you're the only one that truly understands. Can I ask your advice, just one more time? I promise that this will be the last time.'

Jack threw his crutches at her before sitting down. 'You just don't get it, do you? I could've died, Ruby. And you want to lay more of your stress on my head. I'm about to burst—I really am.'

'You told me once that you would do anything for me. Do you hate me so much now that I can't even talk to you? You're the only one, Jack—the only one who gets me.'

'I will always be here for you, Ruby. But you got to slow down. These hair-brain schemes of yours are gonna get us into so much trouble.' He rubbed away at his temples to block out Ruby's plea.

'Jack, this is different. This is about when dad died. Can you remember that the inspector woman took my diary? Well, she still has it. There is stuff in there that will change a lot of things for us. Jack, I can't go through this without you.'

Jack could see how troubled she was. He wanted to walk out the door but couldn't turn his back on her. He sighed, then hugged his sister. The tears that fell from her stone-cold eyes gave no remorse. She had him back where she wanted him; power resumed.

Ruby knew how to manipulate people. At school, she had the teachers wrapped around her fingers. She was naturally clever and didn't need to work on her subjects to get good grades. If she felt she was falling behind in something, she would turn on the charm and get the teacher to accept any lame excuse she offered.

Geography was her worst subject. When she was fifteen, she failed to study for an assignment that would affect her overall exam. Her teacher was in his late twenty's and hadn't been at the school long. After she sweet-talked her way into getting him to give her a lift home from school, she made a move on him. At first, he declined. But she made sure that he had no chance of leaving as she forced herself on top of him. As soon as he gave in and kissed her back, she blackmailed him. The man had been well and truly played. Ruby received an A-plus, and the teacher moved schools. This would be the way Ruby worked. She always got her way no matter who suffered in the long run.

* * *

Heather had been so tied up with the murder investigation and Karen's past, she had put all leads on the counterfeit gang on the back burner. Whilst at the station, the search for Frankie Thompson had moved up a level. They had received a call from a retired police officer saying that they had seen him arguing with someone in a cafe in Newquay.

As Heather arrived, she had to check the address twice. The house was in the corner of a quiet little cul-de-sac, but the windows and doors had shutters on them. It looked like the owner had gone overboard on the security and had barricaded himself in.

A man in his late sixties answered the door, peering through the chain lock. Heather took out her badge and showed it to him through the small opening.

'Hi, Sir, it's DI Williams. I think you may be expecting me.'

After he examined her picture meticulously, he unlocked the chain and had a quick look around before letting her in.

'Are you OK Mr Davies? You seem a little unnerved.'

'Just get inside, will you?' He shut the door and locked it again. 'That Frankie Thompson is a nasty piece of work, and I don't want anyone knowing it was me that tipped you off.'

He led her through to the kitchen and pulled out two mugs from the cupboard.

'I thought he was still banged up, doing time. I nearly dropped my teeth in my tea when I saw him in the cafe earlier. The bloke that was with him didn't seem to take any nonsense from him mind.'

Heather picked up her tea and was promptly shown into the living room. Hanging on the walls were gilded framed photos of Brian Davies in uniform, receiving commendations for police work. Heather smiled. She had found a new respect for the old detective.

'So, tell me, did you hear any of the conversations?'

'I couldn't catch them exactly, but it sounded like a deal going down. They both looked a bit shifty like. He handed over a parcel that was the shape and weight of a brick. Heavy like—he needed two hands to grab it.' He held his hands out to describe his action.

'You could see Frankie's arse was twitching when he received it and then he handed over a bag full of cash. I only glimpsed at it when the bloke checked inside it, but it looked like a lot. I kept my head down after that—didn't want him thinking that I had seen anything.'

Heather noticed a spark in the old detective's eye. She had seen this a lot with ex-police. They never seem to be free of the job, even when retired.

'They both left after that. I saw them drive off in a black BMW—and before you say it, no, I didn't get the reg. A big bastard lorry parked alongside them just as I was about to note it down.'

Heather smiled. 'Don't worry, you have been more than helpful. If you think of anything else or see him again, call me on this number.'

She could see in his expression that he had felt proud of his old coppers' ways once again. As he walked her to the front door he reminisced. Keeping her from leaving straight away.

'I remember Frankie from the old days. He was never one to let an unpaid debt lie. When I was working in

Newport, he had recruited a few of the younger boys, his sons included, to do the drug runs for him. They were all on it at that Beechwood estate. He would start by giving out freebies of the stuff, then when he had got them hooked, he would up the price. He turned most of the kids that he had hooked on it into runners for him to repay their debts. The more they used, the more they had to earn to repay him. It was a vicious circle.'

As she walked back to the car, she heard the door lock firmly behind her.

Heather also remembered Frankie's reign well. When she had worked on the estate, every boy that she arrested for being high or for dealing drugs had Frankie's name attached to it. They would never grass, but you knew early on who was running things. The only trouble was, he kept his nose clean so there would be no proof to be had. Miraculously though, as soon as Frankie was sent down, the influx of drugs stopped. A month later, they started again, and this time it was Wayne Thompson. They had caught him dealing at the school gates to a couple of twelve-year-olds.

The younger brother, Kevin, was no longer a part of the Thompson family. Both of his parents and his brother had disowned him.

Wayne had told Frankie that he found a gay magazine under Kevin's bed. When confronted by Frankie, he said it was because he wanted to look at the pictures when working out. He wanted the same physique as them.

He pleaded with his father and reminded him of all the beatings he had given out to the poofs on the estate. Frankie accepted the excuse, but after that, a few other things didn't add up around the eighteen-year-old. Something had to be done.

Kevin would never admit that he was gay and would do everything he could to be classed as a strong heterosexual Thompson man, respected, and feared by the community. He had a girlfriend that would do anything he said just to stay with him. Frankie paid a rent boy that he had picked up to seduce Kevin and it worked. When the rent boy went to get his money, Frankie hit him so hard in the face that his teeth came through his cheek. Kevin's injuries were worse. Frankie would have no gay son of his anywhere near Newport. After beating the crap out of him, he ordered him to move towns. He hated gays nearly as much as he hated coppers. No son of his would be known as a faggot, as it would hurt his hard man's reputation. He kept telling him he should die of AIDS and forget he ever had a family.

Wayne only kept in contact with his brother to send mail. When their mother had a stroke not long after he left, they blamed the stress of it all on Kevin. She had loved her son and could accept him as a bullying drug dealer but not as a gay boy. She only had one son now and his name was no longer mentioned.

When people asked where Kevin was, Frankie would say that he had been sent down. Although the explanation was so far from the truth, the people that knew Frankie accepted it without a question.

One of Frankie's henchmen told him they had seen Kevin at a Pride March in Cardiff dressed in a Rainbow flag, Dr Martin boots, and gold lycra shorts. The henchman hardly finished his sentence before Frankie slammed his head against the wall, knocking him cleanout.

A month later, they fished his body out of the River Usk. As the police knew him as one of Frankie's men, they didn't look in his direction when making accusations. All they needed from him was to help find out why it happened.

When the police asked Frankie if he had any enemies, he cited the Canton Clan, and the police were happy to accept the suggestion.

The last time they had seen Kevin was when their mother died. She had mentioned him in her will, so he had to attend the reading. Now in dentistry school, he had turned his life around. Regretting with a vengeance at all the things he had done in his youth. He was now in a long-term relationship and living with the man. He hoped and prayed every day that he would never find out about the way he had lived his life.

Learning about his mother's death hit him hard. He hadn't seen or spoken to her since the day he left. The letters he had written were always full of hope. Longing that one day she would contact him back. Accepting his life choices.

His mother, who had been saving her money, left everything to Wayne. Kevin had inherited a teapot. It was a sick dig at his sexuality. She had also left him the pile of unopened letters that he had sent to her. That was the final kick in the teeth. And the last time he had anything to do with his family. He moved back to London with a clear conscience and lived his life without them from that day.

Chapter Twelve

The early morning sun blinded Heather as she pulled into the car park of The Royal Oak pub. As the breakfast menu sign outside came into focus, it made her stomach grumble. But she wasn't there to eat. The pub opposite the cemetery had seemed as good a place as any to piece together a series of events. She looked over at the cemetery. It was a good view from where she was standing. Someone must have seen something, she thought. They had still not established Phil's whereabouts after returning home from Germany to ending up in someone else's grave.

The landlord was sitting at the edge of the bar, tucking into his rather large breakfast. He removed the bar towel he had hanging below his neck and wiped his mouth with it.

The smell of bacon and eggs had hit her as soon as she walked through the door. She couldn't resist, so ordered a breakfast roll before showing him the photo of

Phil. It was a long shot, but one she was glad that she had taken.

'Yeah, I recognise the fella. He came in a couple of weeks ago.' Heather gave him the money for her food. He took the payment, then stopped to think as he was counting the change from the till.

'Let me see. It must have been a Tuesday night as the local ladies camera club were having their weekly meeting.' Heather held out her hand for the change, but the landlord's mind was still elsewhere.

'He had been arguing with a girl in the lounge and they had complained of the girl's language, a fussy lot that camera club. I had to go over there and tell them to simmer down, or they would all have to leave.'

She asked for a description of the girl, but the landlord was quite vague. He said that she had been in her thirties with dark hair. This didn't fit any of the descriptions linked to the case, so she probed more. They had already recorded over the CCTV footage from the pub, so he had to delve into his memory for more information.

'Hang on, I remember more. At the end of the night, the man had passed out, which was strange as I had only served him with a couple of beers.'

'Did you notice them get into a car? Or did they get a taxi or anything?'

'I told them to leave as I was locking up. He could barely stand so another bloke helped her get him to the bench outside. I assume that they would have got a taxi or something, yeah.'

'Thanks, Sir you have been really helpful—here's my card. If you remember anything else, can you let me know?'

The landlord took the card and put it on the noticeboard behind the bar. The local taxi firm was displaying its card for the punters next to it. She called them to see if there had been any pickups from the pub on that Tuesday.

'As I said, Love, there was a taxi booked by a woman but when he arrived, there was no one there. The taxi driver took a walk around the outside of the pub but there was no sign of anyone.'

'Any chance you could give me the taxi driver's name so I can send an officer over to have a chat with him?'

'Yeah, Love, it's Cliffy Harris. He'll be around just before ten, as that's when his shift starts. I'll tell him to be expecting you.'

Heather finished eating her roll then asked the landlord if it was alright to leave her car there when she took a walk over to the cemetery.

'You can walk over there, Love, but that gate won't be open until ten. It gets shut around six every night now as the kids were going in there and vandalising the headstones.'

This was new information for her. They hadn't updated the times on the council website, so she had misjudged the time frame. Whoever got him over there would have had to have been there in daylight.

'What is the quietest time for the cemetery, would you say?'

The landlord shrugged his shoulders. 'Probably when it first opens, I guess. The funerals don't start until eleven, so there will only be a couple of gravediggers around at most.'

Heather got straight on the phone with Gareth and told him to interview the taxi driver. She would spend her day back at the station, checking the CCTV again. There had to be something she was missing. 'Who would he have been arguing with and why?'

When Gareth entered the taxi firm, a few of the drivers recognised him and left. Probably driving illegally or without a taxi licence, he thought. He had bigger fish to fry, so let them carry on, regardless. Cliffy Harris had been waiting. He was a little anxious as time was money and he hated losing the early morning fares.

'Sorry to have kept you, Mr Harris. Bloody traffic this time of the morning is a nightmare.'

'You're telling me about it? You can't make a living when you're stuck at junction twenty-eight waiting for the traffic to ease, bloody ridiculous…'

Gareth interrupted before a full-blown traffic conversation took the place of why he was there.

'So, Mr Harris, can you tell me about the call you had on Tuesday?'

'Well, it was closing time at the Royal Oak. Tuesdays are normally pretty quiet, so I left as soon as the call came in.' He folded up the newspaper that had rested on his lap, leaving ink smudges over his camel-coloured trousers. 'It would only take me ten minutes, as the roads are pretty quiet at that time of night. Especially if you take the lane before..'

Gareth interrupted, 'Mr Harris, can you get to the point, please? I'm sure you want to get back on the road.'

Harris shuffled in his seat and gave Gareth a frown. 'I'm getting to it Mate—I pulled up outside and there was no one around. I walked to the back of the pub to see if anyone was around the back of there being sick—as that happens sometimes but no one. There was a Metro parked at the back with the lights on, so I went over to ask if they had seen anything and there was a guy asleep in the back. I laughed and thought he's had a skin full—then went back to my car and drove off.'

'A Metro, you say. Do you remember what colour?'

'Yeah, it was dark grey, a bit like mine over there,' he pointed to his car that was parked in the taxi bay.

Gareth didn't look up as he was frantically scribbling down the information. 'A stupid question now—you didn't, by any chance, get the registration number?'

Harris laughed. 'Well, as a matter of fact, there was no registration number—well, not at the back, anyway. It had a bump in the back of it, probably a lamppost. I've seen loads like that..'

Gareth stopped him in mid-sentence. This was good information, and he needed to act on it straight away.

'Thank you, Mr Harris, you have been a real help—now get out there and attack that traffic.'

Gareth made a quick escape before being drawn back into another conversation.

He took it upon himself to show some initiative, so he started phoning around the body shops to see if a dark grey Metro had been in for any bodywork. There were a few names flagged up. But nothing to link them with the case. He was about to give up when the last garage he called named a car belonging to Karen Jenkins. At last, he thought. The garage had completed work last week to get the back bumper fixed and replacement number plates added.

It wasn't an offence to get your car fixed and Gareth wondered how he would approach the subject without it sounding too obvious. She had said that she hadn't seen Phil since before Germany yet her car was parked at the scene of the crime. Gareth knew that this was vital evidence and didn't want to approach it on his own. He raced back to the station to talk to Heather about it. The two of them would work out their next move.

Heather listened meticulously to Gareth's news. She was pleased that they had something to go on. 'Well done, Gareth. You have definitely redeemed yourself after leaving the CCTV footage for PC Reid.'

'So, what are your thoughts, Heather? Do you think we could have a jealous wife on our hands here?' Gareth put everything down to jealousy. He was feeling it a little himself since Martha had come back onto the scene. He knew it was ridiculous, as they both had open relationships, but this one was different. Martha always made him feel insecure. He had felt it when Heather mentioned her name. There was always a hint of excitement in her voice.

'I'm not sure Karen is the type, but I think we need to look closer to home if we are to find any answers. Has the family liaison officer noticed anything strange about the family's actions since the death?'

'She said that they were all deeply affected by the loss, but no one as much as Karen. She had taken down his photos as she couldn't bear to look at them, apparently.'

Heather tapped her pen on the desk as her mind ticked over. That reaction could be out of grief or even guilt, she thought. She rose from her chair and picked up her keys. 'Let's get over there and see who has an alibi for that night, shall we?'

When they entered the gate, they could see the Metro parked at the front. The work had been completed, and it looked as good as new. Karen answered the door, and at first, she was pleased to see Heather. Greeting her like an old friend. This changed when she saw Heather's straight face.

'Hi, Karen. Is it OK if we have a quick chat? It won't take long.'

Karen ushered them into the living room and as they passed the kitchen, they could see that Ruby and Jack were both at home. Sitting at the kitchen table.

Gareth began. 'We have reason to believe that Phil went to the Royal Oak pub on the day he got back from Germany. Would you, by any chance, remember where you were on that Tuesday? It's only so we can rule you out of our inquiries. We will also be asking Ruby and Jack the same question.'

Heather rolled her eyes at him for being so abrupt. She didn't want Karen unnerved by any questioning at this early stage. The woman was riddled with grief. It surprised her that, after all this time, Phil's whereabouts were beginning to emerge. She had assumed that it was his demise that had stopped him from returning home to her straight away. This would have been out of his control and easier to accept.

'All I remember is that I was out of my mind with worry. He hadn't come home, and I'd had no calls from him at all, nothing. I remember going to the haulage yard and that Charlie telling me he hadn't seen him. I came home after that and waited by the phone.'

'Do you remember perhaps driving anywhere later that evening?'

'No, definitely not. I stopped driving the car as the number plate kept falling off. I've only just got it fixed since Ruby smashed it up, so I can be sure about that.' Heather looked at Gareth and he raised his eyebrows.

'Does Ruby use your car a lot, Mrs Jenkins?'

'Christ, they all do, even Phil—well did.' She got emotional and swallowed hard. Heather felt her grief and gave her an understanding smile.

'We'll leave it there, for now, Karen. Is it OK for me to go into the kitchen to talk to Ruby and Jack?'

She nodded and led them through. It was too late. Both had left without saying a word.

Karen reached over to her handbag. 'Yup, my keys are gone again. I wouldn't mind, but they never fill it up.'

Heather looked at Gareth. He knew what she was thinking and left to start the car.

'You wouldn't by any chance know where they may be going, would you? Or what time they would be back?'

Karen shook her head. 'Your guess is as good as mine with them two Love. But Jack won't be going far. He's still having terrible headaches from falling off his bike. It's affecting him more than he's telling me, I'm sure.' She walked over to the fridge. 'Maybe they've popped to the shop. I know we're out of milk.'

Heather thanked Karen and told them she would be in touch.

Gareth pushed open the door for Heather. 'Shall we find them—get them in for questioning?'

'Not just yet. I don't want to scare them off. Let's leave it for now and see what turns up.'

* * *

Martha had finished bathing the dogs. And they were drying off in the cellar next to the wood boiler. It was time to take a break. Sitting on the veranda in her favourite chair overlooking the sea, she sipped her coffee. She had always wanted a place to escape to, and this had been an absolute bargain. It may have been falling apart and sea weathered, but it was her home.

The details of Heather's case were still laying heavily on her mind. There still hadn't been a good time to tell her about meeting up with Ruby. Every time she went to pick up the phone, she would dial the number, then put it down again before she answered. There were no words.

She had made a huge mistake in not letting a full investigation take place and would have to put things right. Ruby was hiding something, and she knew it. Why did she want the past to stay dead? What did ten-year-old Ruby see? Heather would have to be told. It was unfair to keep this information away from her investigation.

She thought about the time she had shared with Heather. The passion they had for each other was still as intense as when they had first met. If only she hadn't been so career-driven in the past, she could be sitting here with her now, she thought. Instead of alone reminiscing about the mistakes she had made.

The wind was picking up, and the waves were whipping against the sea wall with brute force. With the large doors open to the elements, the spray was drifting into the room; dampening the furniture.

As she stood to close them, she noticed a reflection on the glass of a figure standing behind her.

She quickly stepped to the right of the veranda and over the wall into the next room.

Arming herself with the fire poker, she gently opened the door. As she moved into the hallway, she could feel the presence of someone behind. She turned and lashed out with the poker, but missed the intruder. The figure ran into the living room and Martha gave chase to the best of her ability. The room was full of little nooks for hiding places, and she was now spinning in circles, debating which way to turn.

After a minute, which had felt more like ten, she walked over to the veranda. Looking down into the garden, she noticed the back gate swaying in the wind. Whoever it was, she must have scared them off, she thought.

There had been a spate of burglaries in the area recently. She had helped a neighbour further down the beach to report an incident only last week. The police were moving the druggies away from the streets to clean up their appearance. They were now hanging around the beach. Hiding behind the rocks to get their fix. It was probably the same bunch of wasters, she thought.

She was proud of herself for how she had handled the situation. And smiled as she bent down to put the poker back onto its hook. She stumbled. The blow she received on the back of her head almost had her unconscious. As she lay in a pool of her own blood, her eyes flickered. She could see a blurry figure ripping her beautiful home apart. She closed her eyes.

Chapter Thirteen

Heather took her coffee from the machine and was about to take a well-earned sip before PC Reid bounded towards her.

'DI Williams there was a message left for you at the desk from the landlord of the Royal Oak. He asked if you could go over there straight away Ma'am.'

Heather looked at her coffee then gave the cup to PC Reid.

The Royal Oak looked busy for a Tuesday. Plenty of punters enjoying an early evening pint after work. She looked over their heads to the bar and caught sight of the landlord. He was busy pulling a pint but signalled with his head for her to join him.

'Good. You made it. The camera club are in.' He gave the man his pint and walked to the end of the bar.

'It's the same girls that were here that night, give or take a few.'

He pointed over at them. They had pushed two tables together to make a big one. Various photos were laid out before them and the women were deep in conversation, discussing style and form.

'The thing is DI Williams when I went over there to collect the glasses, I noticed that the geezer you were asking about was on one of the photos. Take a look, the ladies won't mind.'

She introduced herself and asked to scan over the tables collection. After a few grumbles and questions about why she needed to, they let her peruse freely. The landlord was right. Phil was in two of the photos. One of them clearly showed him sitting at the table with a pint in front of him. The other, presumably taken a little later, had him slumped in a chair looking the worst for wear. You couldn't see his face clearly by the positioning, but it was definitely him.

Next to him was a female wearing a loose beanie hat. As Heather examined it closer, she could see that it was Ruby. She looked like she was in a conversation with another man. Got you, she thought.

The girls let her take the photos as evidence and she promised them a round at the bar. She showed the photo once again to the barman and pointed out the man talking to Ruby.

'Any idea who this is?'

The landlord squinted, then realised who it was.

'That's Dai, the cemetery caretaker. He's always in here after work. I think he's outside now having a fag.'

The smoking area overlooked the cemetery. A young man was sitting on the bench drawing the last out of a rolly.

Heather introduced herself by flashing her police badge. He was a bit startled at first, as he was an honest boy and not one that had been used to a police presence.

'Hey, Dai. Is it OK if I sit down and have a quick word with you?'

He slid down the seat to make room and looked at her, confused.

'I haven't done nuffin' wrong, have I?'

Heather smiled. Although the man was in his twenties, he still had the face of a child.

'No Dai—at least I don't think so. Can you remember seeing this man or this lady in the pub a few weeks back?' she showed Dai the photo's, and he reacted instantly.

'Yes, I do—that's the girl who helped me find my keys. I always put them on the table by my coat after I've locked the cemetery gates. I can't carry my pint to the table otherwise see.'

He lifted his pint in the air, then took a sip

'I drank my pint, then I couldn't find them anywhere. It was like they just disappeared. I was looking everywhere for them.'

Heather was now the one looking confused.

'What, the lady and the man?'

'No, silly my keys.' He giggled at Heather's mistake. 'It was like they just disappeared. I was looking everywhere for them. Then later when I gave up looking, that girl said she found them under my chair and gave them to me.' He shook his head. 'But I know I looked under my chair. It was really strange.'

'Dai, do you think that there may have been a chance that she would have taken the keys? Had you seen the girl before?'

Dai screwed his face up in disbelief. 'She saw me locking the gate as she was sitting here where you are now. So why would she want to take them? It's not like they are for a big car or sumfin.'

'No Dai, you're right. What would a girl like that want with keys to a cemetery?'

She thanked him and paid the landlord for his next pint for his trouble.

'I'm gonna be skint by the time I leave here. But thanks for calling me in it's been most helpful.'

She grabbed a twenty-pound note from her purse and handed it over to him. The landlord looked at it twice and felt the paper. He took out a fraud detector pen and scored the note. It turned brown, and he gave it back to her.

'You should know better than that Love, that's a dodgy twenty. We've had loads of them turn up in here over the last couple of weeks.'

She swapped the note for a new one and apologised for her mistake.

As she walked back to the car, she took out her mobile to arrange for a car to pick up Ruby. She needed her down at the station to make a statement about that night and didn't want to warn her beforehand. Before she could dial the number, the phone went off in her hand.

'Chief Inspector Morris—What can I do for you, Sir?'

'Heather, I need you to pay a visit to Cardiff nick to have a little chat with Ramsgate. A new batch of counterfeit twenties has turned up. There must be at least £20k.'

She told her boss about the one she had in her purse and he asked her to check the serial number before explaining what had happened.

'We've had two Japanese tourists in worrying that the money they won at the casino last night were fakes. They were right. £20k in twenty-pound notes with the same serial numbers as the last lot.'

Heather sat in the car and put her phone on speaker. She held her twenty up to the light and examined it carefully. It was pretty good, she thought. She wouldn't have known if the landlord hadn't said.

'So, has the casino been laundering them then?'

'No evidence of that yet. According to them, it must have come in from a customer. Get down there and see if Ramsgate has any idea where they may have come from.'

* * *

The cold grey gates closed behind her. Echoing against the breeze blocks. After being checked in and frisked by the officer in charge, they led her to the visitors room. As Ramsgate came in, she hardly recognised him. He had lost at least two stone in weight and the unshaven look didn't suit him. He had faded orange blush bruises about his face and hands, accompanied by a fresh cut sitting across the top of his nose.

'Inspector Williams, how lovely of you to pay me a visit.'

He screeched a chair across the floor before sitting down, putting Heather's teeth on edge.

'OK, Ramsgate cut the crap. You know this isn't a friendly visit.'

He smiled. Then put on a straight, judgemental face.

'If you think I'm gonna give you any more information for nothing, you're out of your mind. Look at the state of me. I'm getting regular beatings in here for being your grass…'

Heather interrupted. 'Now hang on a minute, Mate. It was you that offered the information for a lighter sentence and you know it. Don't go blaming us because your popularity has failed.'

If the con was looking for a scapegoat. This was good, Heather thought. He may give out some information, especially if she could put a little deal on the table.

'Just make it quick, will you. They will nick my fucking stuff if I don't hurry the thieving bastards. Well—what do you want?'

Heather felt like making him wait for being so disrespectful. But she wanted to get out of that stinking place, too.

'There has been a new flow of counterfeit cash circulating the casino. You said that was the last stash. If that was so, how come there are at least £20k of bent twenty-pound notes sitting in the station as we speak?'

Ramsgate's eyes darted between Heather and the lump of a prison guard that was minding the door. She took the hint and asked if the prison guard could stand outside for a little while. He gave Ramsgate an ice-cold stare as he passed him. He would pay for this action when he got back.

Heather took her mobile out to record the conversation.

'Right, talk. And you better not be bullshitting me.'

Ramsgate sat further back into his chair and folded his arms.

'I'll talk when you put a deal in front of me and not before.'

She shook her head. 'How do I know that you're not gonna feed me a load of spiel?' Heather had been in this position before with Ramsgate. He was fond of giving her half a story.

He shrugged at her comment. Heather would need some quick thinking.

'What if I can get you moved out of here? Away from Thompson's men. Surely that would be tempting enough for you to open that big mouth of yours.'

Ramsgate paused for a while, then unfolded his arms. He sat up straight to listen, pulling his feet underneath him.

'Go on.'

'Well, as long as you've had no disciplinary's in the time you've been here, I might be able to arrange a move.'

'Disciplinary's nah not me Mate. Model prisoner I am. Look, I may have something for you. I didn't want to mention the guy's name before, but—hey. If I'm getting my arse beaten for him, then it's not really fair, is it?'

He looked around to make sure the guard wasn't watching him through the little round window. Then leaned in close to reveal his information.

'You need to speak to Phil Jenkins. He used to drive the lorry for me. He had more money stashed away, and he was also the go-between man for the plates.'

Heather sat staring for a while, not knowing whether to mention that Phil was now deceased. It surprised her to hear his accusations. And doubted his story about the man being so deeply involved. She didn't trust a word that came out of Ramsgate's mouth unless she had the proof to confirm it. The chief wouldn't be happy if it turned out to be a pack of lies either.

If that was all he had on offer, then it wouldn't justify a transfer. She decided she had no other choice than to give it to him straight.

'Jenkins is dead, so using him as your get out of jail card will not work.'

Ramsgates' face was like a rabbit caught in headlights. It stopped him in his tracks.

'Dead? How come nobody told me? Poor Phil.'

After a few seconds' silence, he gave his view on the situation. 'Thompson's bastards are everywhere, so it's not surprising. Pity though, he was a good mate—and having a hard enough time at home as it was.'

It was Heather's time to sit up and listen.

'How do you know it was, Thompson? Are you sure you know nothing else?'

Ramsgate was certain. And raised his voice to get his point across.

'It must have been him. He didn't have any enemies as he was a nice guy, except for his nut-case of a stepdaughter.'

The mention of Ruby by an outsider had Heather excited to question more.

'What do you know about their relationship?'

'Well, that was the point. There was no relationship. But that Ruby was obsessed with him. He was halfway to Germany once, and he found her stowed away in the cab. She would have made it all the way too if she hadn't trapped her scarf in the door.'

'How do you know all this?'

Ramsgate rolled his eyes.

'Well, I had a massive go at him for being late, and that was the excuse he gave me. It was lucky that he stopped for a piss and saw it blowing in the wind or she would have made it to Germany. The scarf belonged to her mother, which made it even worse for Phil to cope with. He had to take the girl all the way back home. He nearly missed the drop-off.'

'So, there was definitely no affair then?'

'Christ no. His family meant the world to him. Especially his stepson. He used to travel with him sometimes on trips to Germany. He seemed like a good bloke, a little quiet, but you could tell he was all there like.'

Heather turned off her phone recording and got her stuff together. Ramsgate shuffled uncomfortably in his chair as if he was waiting to be fed a crumb of food.

'Woh, woh, where are you going? What about our deal? Am I getting a transfer or what?'

Heather didn't answer straight away and knocked on the door to be let out.

'I'll be back in a day or two. Have another think of what you can offer us, and I'll have a word with the chief.'

At last, she had a suspect with a motive. Ruby's name had come up twice in conjunction with the disappearance of Phil. There were a lot of loose ends to follow.

When they finally tracked Ruby down, she was complaining heavily that she had nothing of any interest to tell them. But when Heather showed her the photo of her sitting alongside Phil in the pub, she soon changed her story.

'Ruby, the question is straightforward enough. Why did you not mention to anyone that you saw Phil before he died?'

The girl twisted a tissue nervously in her hand. She had used it to wipe away the fake tears laid on to impress Heather.

'You won't like what I have to say. The man was a paedo. He had groomed me from an early age.'

She forced out a few more fake tears before continuing with a shaky drawl.

'He invited me to the pub to say that he had been sorry for his actions over the years.'

Heather made sure her doubts were clear. She wouldn't succumb to manipulation by her.

'Ruby, if this is true, why haven't you told your mother about this? And why did you stowaway in Phil Jenkins' cab to Germany a few weeks back?'

Ruby's frustration was visible. She tripped over her words as she tried to answer.

'I didn't stowaway. If you must know, he tried to kidnap me. Look, if you don't believe me, ask Jack. He knows what type of man he was.'

Ruby put her head down and sobbed. 'Please don't tell my mother about any of this. She's been through enough and wouldn't be able to cope.'

It was obvious to Heather that she was lying. But with no hard evidence, she couldn't prove it. She held back on suggesting that she had anything to do with Phil's murder, as she didn't want her to wriggle out of the questions. She would see what her brother had to say. And see if he could give her a lead to suspect her as a killer.

Jack was even harder to track down than Ruby. Heather had left several messages on his phone for him to contact her, but no reply. Karen was having the same problem. She didn't know where he was. It had been a week since she had heard from him and worried about his wellbeing. She enlisted the help of Heather to break into his flat for clues.

By the look of the mail piled up next to the door, Jack hadn't been there in quite a while. When they went into the bedroom, they noticed that all of his clothes had gone. This worried Karen, but at least it meant that he had probably left on his own accord, she thought.

On the table were several bits of paper. It had details of flights flying out from Cardiff to Germany. According to Karen, this was out of character for Jack. He always told his mother if he was going away anywhere. It worried her that the bang on his head may have been changing his character.

Heather needed him to collaborate with Ruby's story. Until then, she would treat Ruby as her prime suspect. Although Ramsgate had pointed the finger at Thompson, Heather still wasn't sure that burying him on top of a grave would be his thing.

* * *

When Martha opened her eyes, everything in front of them was spinning. As she reached up to touch her pounding head, she felt the sticky blood matted through her hair. You've been in worse situations than this girl, she thought. And pushed down hard on her muscular arms to get into some sort of sitting position. The curtains had been tightly closed. It was hard to see her way around the furniture. She crawled around the floor, patting with her hands, hoping to find the wire attached to the phone. As her blood-stained fingers located it, she pulled it from the side table to the floor.

She knew Heather was the last person to call her, so squinting to locate the button, she pressed the return call.

Heather was reluctant to answer at first. It had been a few days since their rendezvous and she hadn't heard from her. She had wanted to make the call herself but was determined not to go back to the way it used to be. A one-sided relationship with only her making any effort.

'Hey Martha, you took your time to call me back. I felt a bit of a booty call, just like the old days.' The phone was silent. Then Heather could make out her struggling to breathe. 'Martha—Martha. Are you OK?'

Martha tried to tell her what had happened but was having trouble with getting the words out. All she could manage was to ask for help. 'No police — just you— please Heather.'

Luckily for Martha, Heather was not that far away. She was following another lead on Frankie.

She put her foot down as fast as she could through the mountain edged roads and got to Martha's within fifteen minutes of the call.

As she approached the house, the gate was still swinging on its hinges. Someone had turned her quaint little house upside down. Martha's attempt to phone her was visible on the floor. Bloodstains smeared the off the hook handset, and it looked like someone had dragged her across the floor.

She searched the house but couldn't find her. After shining her torch around the living room, she noticed sitting on top of an open black holdall, a pink diary from 2000. She took it out and glanced over its cover quickly. She undid the clasp and read the inside cover. This book belongs to Chloe. Keep out. The book fell open at an entry that had been just before Craig Lewis's death.

I am never ever letting Ruby come over to play anymore as she always steals my things. I told her what my daddy does to me when my mummy goes out and she told me I was lying. I even showed her my pictures, but she just laughed at me. Her daddy gives her everything, and he is lovely to her. I wish my daddy was like that. She is always nasty to him. I wish he was my daddy.

The hand-drawn pictures inside were hard to miss and sickened her stomach. A neat wad of twenty-pound notes lined the inside of the holdall, giving her the realisation that the intruder may still be there. She quickly dropped the book back into the bag and contemplated her next move.

The stillness of the house gave way to footsteps. The bag was still in view and Heather looked frantically for a hiding spot. She hid behind the living room curtain and quickly texted Gareth to bring silent back up. If she could hold her cool and not be noticed, she would soon get a look at who it belonged to and continue the search for Martha.

The minutes felt like hours as the intruder opened and closed doors, but her wait wasn't in vain. She put her hand over her mouth, desperately trying not to make any sound as she saw the dark figure getting closer. It was too early for Gareth to have made it and as the occasional breeze took hold of the thin curtain material; she was regretting her choice of hiding spot.

In the darkness of the living room, she trembled. Gazing warily through the crack in the curtains, she held her breath as the figure walked into the kitchen and over to the fridge. As he opened the door to take out a bottle of milk, she could clearly see from the light of the fridge it was Jack.

There was still no sign of Martha and Heather was fearing for her life.

After chugging down the milk, he took out a plate of cold chicken and placed it on the table. He was close enough to touch her as he bounded in, grabbed the bag, and took it back to the kitchen. He rammed a piece of chicken into his mouth, wiped his hand on his trousers, then took the book out of the bag. It was at that moment that she realised she had forgotten to put the clasp back together and prayed he wouldn't notice. He flicked at it back and forth as the suspense of him realising caused Heather's beads of sweat to drip down her face. She was lucky.

As he opened it, the book revealed the owner's name inside the cover again. As Jack flicked menacingly through the pages, he shuffled on the chair in frustration. The words that Ruby had written, and showed him the night that his father had died, pulled on his memory. These and the graphic children's art she showed him had convinced the boy that his father was a monster.

He stood up and paced the floor. After studying the words, he realised poor Chloe had been the one being abused every night. Not Ruby. She had used his gullibility to her own advantage. It wasn't her tale to tell.

'Bitch. Fucking lying bitch.' He shouted loud enough for the glasses that were stacked up on the kitchen drainer to rattle. He smashed at the contents of the table as he pushed them with force onto the floor. He sat back down and battled against the tears that appeared in his eyes, wiping them hard with his sleeve.

After a logical moment, a calm seemed to wash over him. He picked up his phone and started mumbling into it. She tried with all her might to hear the conversation, but only caught the last few sentences as he picked up his jacket from the living room.

'Just bring me the fucking money and you can have the book.'

As he listened to the receiving voice, Heather could see through the curtain gap the grimace on his face as he tried to stay calm.

'Just meet me in the car park in two hours and don't forget to bring the money. No money. No book—do you hear?' And then he left.

Heather waited until she heard his motorbike roar off into the distance. She ran to Martha's room and took out her gun from the bedroom drawer. She had known it was there when she was looking for something to tie Martha's arms to the bedpost.

With a gun in hand and a careful eye, she followed the bloodstains out of the patio doors and down the garden path to the beach. Martha was lying out on the sand with hands stretched out like Christ. The waves had not yet reached her. Another half-hour would have given a different story. The tide would have taken her out to sea.

The thought of a world without Martha overwhelmed Heather. She gently peered over her, looking for signs of trauma. The shadow on her skin made Martha open her eyes.

'You took your time, woman.'

Heather smiled at her. And held her tight in her arms; cradling her old love as if it had been their first embrace. She could feel dampness as her hand filled up with the blood seeping through her hair.

'Hold on Martha. Don't you leave me!'

She wiped away her tears, then ripped off her sleeve to stem the flow, wrapping it as tight as she could without damaging the wound even more.

As Gareth and PC Reid trudged through the sand to the beach, they sped up when they saw the two women sitting on the sand. Gareth tried to make sense of the scenario and pointed to the gun that was lying on the floor.

'Christ, have they shot her?'

'No—at least I don't think so. That's Martha's gun. I remembered seeing it in her bedside drawer, so I brought it out here in case she wasn't alone.'

Gareth cocked his eyes. 'Why doesn't that surprise me?'

Heather gave a wry smile back. He was right. Whenever Martha was around, she couldn't help herself. They had a connection, and he knew he would never be enough for her.

'I saw who it was, Gareth. It was Jack Lewis. We need to get the whole force out looking for him.'

She grabbed the sleeve on his jacket and brought him down to her.

'It's not just for the attack on Martha. Ruby had a book, containing evidence to do with Craig Lewis's death. This could be the key to both murders.'

As the ambulance arrived and the paramedics took Martha from Heather, she stopped breathing. They quickly lay her down and began CPR. Heather screamed at Gareth to get back out there and look for Jack. He couldn't get away with this.

As Gareth left, he took PC Reid in tow. The young PC had been by his side throughout the investigation. He was very handsome and had turned Gareth's head on the odd occasion.

'Where do we begin? We are miles away from any cameras.'

'We start by phoning it in my boy, then every inch of these lanes will be scoured by South Wales' finest.'

Chapter Fourteen

Ruby was pleased to see Jack as he picked her up as promised. But Jack couldn't bring himself to look at her. She had always been the only person in his life that he could count on, but it was all a lie. The memory Jack had of his sister from the night that his father died was always at the forefront of his mind. It shrouded her whole narcissistic personality from him. He had lived with the regret of leaving Ruby alone to suffer that night. Blaming himself for the outcome. Ruby knew this. And she had made sure that he had been at her beck and call ever since. He was her protector. Preventing anyone from ever saying a bad word about her.

'So, did you get the book?'

As the words fell out of her mouth, he felt his stomach turn. That book had changed everything. Just as she said it would. She had told him not to look inside; insisting that the contents would upset him. But he did.

And things were not as he had expected. She had not been a victim of abuse. It was the girl next door, Chloe, and her father. Craig Lewis had died for nothing.

'Just get on the back and we'll go somewhere quiet to talk.'

She sat astride the bike and held on tight to Jack's waist. They ploughed through the winding lanes of the Welsh valleys at speed. Dodging some potholes and purposely bumping through the others.

All he could think about was how her evil hands that were around his waist could easily release with a swerve of the bike. He wanted to shake her off and leave her under a truck somewhere as he thought about the fathers she had taken away from him.

'Slow down, Jack, you're gonna kill us both.'

He didn't care. Even if the uneven curves of the country roads took him with it, he didn't care. He had lost all sense of what was right in his life. He revved up the engine and sped the bike around the corners. The girl was hanging on with fear as he weaved dangerously through the traffic. He took a corner too wide, and an oncoming vehicle swerved out of the way at the last second, smashing his horn with malice.

'Jack—please stop—I want to get off!'

Ruby had thought about jumping, but the speed was too fast for her to make it in one piece. He was driving too close to the edge, and she could see the drop inches away from the front tyre.

He slowed down as they reached the top of the mountain road. He pulled his bike to the side, allowing his sister to get off.

Ruby went ballistic. Frantically brushing herself down whilst screaming into his face.

'What the fuck were you doing? You could have killed us, you stupid twat.'

Jack took off his helmet and just stared at the girl. There were no words to share with someone so vile and unhinged. He had loved his sister more than anyone else in his life, and she had used him. He sat on the hillside and let the cool evening air blow into his face.

Ruby was getting restless. It had been at least ten long minutes, and he still hadn't spoken.

'Jack—Jack—what the fuck do you think you're doing? We need to get back home and burn that book before it comes back to bite us in the arse.'

Jack turned and shook his head. 'Bites you in the arse, Ruby—you—not me.'

The girl put her hands firmly on her hips as if to correct him as a parent.

'Ahem, we are in this together, Jack. Remember? What's my problem is your problem. That's what you said to me.'

Jack stood up, still shaking his head. He could see now what everybody else saw. A selfish brat that only ever thought of herself.

'Ruby—poor deluded Ruby. You played me right from the beginning. You were ten-years-old and knew exactly how to manipulate the situation. Why? That's all I want to know is why?'

'What are you talking about? The man was abusing me, Jack, you know that.'

Jack didn't want to look at her, so spoke to the ground.

'But he wasn't Ruby. I looked at your precious book. Poor fucking Chloe next door was getting abused every night by her waster of a father—not you. You were just getting told off now and then for being a complete and utter little shit.'

Ruby bounded towards him. And stamped her feet.

'How dare you! Dad used to slap my legs and send me to my room—with no food mind. That's abuse.'

Jack looked up at her. Her eyes were now as black as her hair.

'Ruby, Ruby, you stupid girl.'

He stood up and steadied himself on the grass. After staring into her lifeless eyes, he put his hands around her throat and lifted her off the ground.

'All this time, you have controlled me—and I fell for it.'

He held his grip tighter around her throat. Her feet desperately tried to scramble away from the edge. He let go of her, causing her to fall backwards and over the edge of the 300-foot drop below. Jack never looked down. As he walked away, he heard the crack of her back as she landed.

He had never wanted to hurt anyone. It was all because of her. He had made bad choices and done things he had regretted, but this year he was about to put it all behind him. There would be no chance of that now. He would be on the run. He missed Phil and his wise advice.

If only he had woken up to Ruby sooner, he thought. Then Phil would have still been alive.

Ruby was the one to blame, and now she had paid. There was one more debt to collect and that would be the end of all his pathetic past. He could make a new life for himself, in Germany or somewhere. He liked it there. It reminded him of Phil.

Jack drove under the bypass and into the car park. As expected, it was empty in the day, apart from a few homeless tents cwtched away in dark corners. The smell of damp piss left by last night's club-goers filled his nostrils. He drove to the top level, and the revs from his engine disturbed the silence. He looked over to the solitary car parked at the end of the bay. It would be over soon.

He parked his bike in the bay opposite, with the book safely locked away in his bike box.

The car door opened and Frankie Thompson, Chloe Fisher's father, got out of the car. He had lived next door to them on the estate after he had split up with his ex, Wayne and Kevin's mother. His new girlfriend Joan had Chloe not long after. She and Ruby were close friends and always in one another's houses.

He reached into his inside pocket.

'Don't even think about pulling a gun on me, Frankie. I have photos of that book and your sick fucking paedo ways in an email that if anything happens to me, will go straight to the police.'

Frankie stood quietly, looking at him. Who did this little boy think he was talking to? he thought. He would play the game until he had the book in his possession.

'Calm down, son. I'm just lighting my cigar. Do you want one?'

He held out a cigar to Jack, and the boy knocked it to the floor.

'Don't you dare call me son! I saw it Frankie—I saw what you did—you're sick.'

He spat at the old man's feet, knowing that he was sailing close to getting a slap. He couldn't stop himself. He had opened that can of nastiness and had too much to say.

'When you lived next door to us on the estate, I looked up to you. I used to listen from my bedroom window to you telling my dad over the fence about all your gangster ways. Everyone feared you, but I didn't.'

He bounced back and forth with restless feet. He wanted to slap the old man, but he knew he wouldn't survive it.

'So did you kill him, Frankie? Did you kill my dad?'

Frankie looked confused. He screwed his wrinkly face up and conveyed his innocence.

'No, I never son—Jack. I liked your old man. He was an OK bloke.'

Jack was still raw with grief. He kept bouncing on his feet, then pointed into the old man's face.

'All this time. I thought it was you—I even thanked you for doing it under my breath. I thought you had killed him to save Ruby from all the shit. When all the time you were abusing Chloe. Ruby was just being selfish…'

Frankie had had enough. He wasn't used to being talked down to like this and didn't like it. He wouldn't put up with it anymore.

'You have no fucking proof, kid. What you told me—that was in that book. It's all lies from a spoilt brat. Your sister was the same. She was fucking mental even back then, always screaming the place down like an alley cat.'

On any other day, Jack would have killed to protect his sister, but now he hated her more than anyone. She had lied to him. She had told him what she wanted him to hear so he could hate his father and spend more time with her. He had worked it out on his way over that this had probably been the problem with Phil as well. They had gone to Germany together and had been getting a close bond. He hated the thought of her now.

Frankie could see the boy was in no fit state to listen, so tried to spell it out for him.

'Calm down, will you, and listen to me carefully? The day your dad died, I was in the clink. Ask around—anyone will tell you. It was the start of my ten-year sentence.'

Jack had thought that Frankie had made himself disappear after killing his father for Ruby. He had thought of him as a hero. His whole life had been a sequence of lies on top of lies.

'Look, son—all this reminiscing is nice and all, but where's the fucking book?'

Jack felt the bile rise into his mouth as he went back to his bike to get the book.

'Throw me the money and you can have the book.' He held it up in his hand and Frankie put a bag full of money out in front of him.

Jack looked over at the bag. 'I'll be checking that money mind and it had better be Kosher. I made those printing plates, don't forget, so I know the difference between the real thing and the counterfeit shit that we've been turning out.'

Frankie threw the £10k over to him and Jack sifted through, checking the serial numbers as he went ahead.

Frankie tutted at his lack of trust for him.

'It's real—don't worry—and those printing plates that you handed over in the cafe had better be the last set. That fucking DI Williams has been sniffing around again and asking questions about me.'

It was the last lot. Phil had kept that set to bargain with, if the cops had ever come knocking at his door. The plan would be to find a bent copper and use them as a bargaining tool to get him and Jack in the clear. There was always one lurking in the background that would do anything for a good set of dodgy printing plates. He knew that if he used them as payment, a good bent copper would leave their names out of any investigation.

Frankie started the engine. He pulled over to Jack to divulge one last piece of information.

'You better tell that slut Ruby to keep her mouth shut about us as well. She wanted it just as much as Chloe and didn't mind taking money from me either. Especially when it became a regular thing. Thanks for the book, Jack.'

As he watched Frankie drive away, the reality about what he had done to Ruby hit him flat in the face. Yes, she had lied to him, but she was only ten-years-old and being abused by Frankie as well. No wonder she was so messed up.

When Phil came along and took them off the estate, Ruby had seemed so happy. But as she grew into a mixed-up young woman, Phil didn't stand a chance. Not reciprocating her infatuation with him became his downfall. Ruby didn't deserve to die. She needed help, and he had let her down again.

That perverted bastard can't get away with this, he thought. He should pay. Jack would have to do the right thing at least once to ease his conscience, or there would be no point in carrying on.

Chapter Fifteen

Tuesday

'Jack, listen I need your help. Get Mam's car and meet me at the Royal Oak, OK.'

Ruby put the phone down and left the queue of people waiting to phone taxis. As she squeezed her way past and sat back down next to Phil, the landlord tutted.

'Come on, you lot, time to leave. Ain't, you got homes to go to?' He buzzed around in his sweat-filled shirt with his beer belly hanging over his trousers. It had been a busy night and all he wanted to do was get home. But trying to get everyone to vacate the pub was taking ages.

Phil was flat out and slumped in the chair. His head was so heavy he could barely lift it on waking. Ruby was kicking his chair with her foot and shaking him in his seat. He came around for a few minutes but couldn't focus.

'Phil, we got to go. Drink the rest of that pint down. I need to go to the ladies. Come on, Jack will be here in a minute.'

She picked up his pint and swirled the rest of the Valium in the bottom to make sure it disappeared with the last of the dregs. She held his head back and poured it down his throat. He slumped back in his chair, and she kicked him once again before she left.

The queue for the toilet was full of the camera club girls and Ruby was getting restless. She pushed her way through and banged on the doors.

'For fuck's sake, hurry up, will you? How long does it take to shake your lettuce?'

The ladies from the club gave Ruby a knowing glare. She had already been told off once that night by the landlord. He had warned her about her language. Now all she wanted was for the fucking fat arse camera club women to fuck off home.

Everything was in place. She had opened the cemetery gate, and all she needed to do was to get the useless bastard over there and bury him.

When she came back from the toilets, she saw Jack had arrived.

She looked over at him and greeted him with a smile that meant she was about to get him into some sort of trouble.

She had sunk quite a few whiskeys herself and was shushing him even before he said anything to her.

'Shh, come and see who I've got here.'

As Jack saw Phil, he couldn't believe how gullible it had made him feel. He had told Ruby that her infatuation with him was all in her head and he had convinced himself that it was. So why was he pissed as a fart and alone with her? he thought.

'Ruby, why the fuck have you brought me in on this—I don't want to get involved. Fine, you're shagging him, I believe you, but what the fuck has it got to do with me?'

Jack turned to leave. As he passed Phil to take the door to the car park, Phil grabbed Jack's leg. He desperately tried to get his attention. If only he could mouth the words to explain to him what was going on, Jack could help. But his limbs were not working properly. Neither was his mouth. It was as if he had swallowed a bag of cotton wool.

Jack kicked him off as he tried to pull himself up, grabbing at his jeans. He tumbled to the floor. It surprised Jack that Phil had noticed him. He picked him up and pushed him back into his seat. His head was continually swaying from side to side, but there was a slight recognition of contact.

'You keep your hands off me. I'm not being your crutch after what you've done to Mam. She was like your fucking daughter, you dirty bastard.'

He shouted in his ears, but the look of confusion on his face and the glare in his eye over rid any rational thought. Ruby sighed, disapproving of Jack's statement.

'Just help me get him in the car, will you?'

He looked at the drunken mess and shook his head.

'No fucking way,' he scoffed. 'It's your mess. You deal with it. I'm off.'

Ruby pulled Jack to the side. 'You said that you would always be there for me. It's not how it looks, Jack. I didn't want any of this. I came home from school one day and he just pounced on me.'

'No—no, I don't believe you, not Phil. This would have been your doing. I know what you're like.'

She showed him a photo on her phone of Ruby kissing Phil.

'That proves nothing. The man looks asleep. What are you trying to do to us?'

She grabbed his sleeve and pulled him for a closer look at Phil.

'Well, how do you explain all this, then?'

She pointed at Phil, who had now completely passed out.

'He's here, isn't he? You saw the texts that I sent him. If he wasn't interested in me, he wouldn't be here, would he?'

Jack let his thoughts take hold. He was feeling the hatred towards Phil burn up in his entire body.

'Just grab him under the arms and help me get him outside.'

They sat him on the bench and argued over what to do next.

'I'll chuck him in the car. Then I'm ordering him a taxi. I'm not driving that perverted bastard anywhere. He can wait in the car, but that's it.'

By the time the taxi had arrived, everyone else had left. Phil was fast asleep on the back seat, and Jack had wandered off into the pub gardens to think. He watched as the taxi drove off, so made his way back to the car. Phil was still inside.

'Why is he still here? I told you to put him in the taxi.'

'I wanted to explain to you, Jack. You don't understand what this dirty bastard is like. They are all the same.'

Ruby kissed her brother on the side of his cheek.

'Except for you, Jack, you're the only one I can trust.'

Jack pushed her away. And wiped his cheek.

'Well, he can't stay in there all night, can he? And like I said, I ain't taking him home.'

Ruby was about to put her plan in place. She had annoyed Jack enough that he would do anything to get out of this situation.

'What about over there?' She pointed to the cemetery, and Jack looked at her as if she was crazy.

'We can't do that—can we?' The boy was angry and didn't want to be involved anymore.

'Why not? Mam doesn't know he's back yet, so no one will miss him. Let the dirty bastard wake up in there tomorrow and hopefully, he'll shit himself so much that he won't wanna come back.'

They drove him in through the gate. Then carried him under the arms to the graveside. They thought it would be apt to leave him by their dad's grave. So laid him flat out by the side of a fresh grave behind.

'That's it. I'm off.'

Jack went to walk back to the car, but Ruby stopped him and pulled him back.

'Let's bury the fucker.'

She got down on her knees and moved the flowers that were laid out in sympathy. The ground was soft, and Ruby pawed her way like a dog with a bone. Sinking her hands into the fresh earth that was lying on top of the newly dug grave.

It wasn't happening fast enough for her, so she ran over to the caretaker's shed that she had unlocked earlier. She took out a shovel and threw it over to Jack. He jumped out of the way as it nearly hit him.

'No fucking way. This is taking it too far. We only want to scare him.'

Ruby picked it up and reminded Jack once again that it was Phil's fault for grooming her. He reluctantly took it from her and started digging.

'Aw Ruby, I don't like this. I might hit the fucking coffin.'

'Don't be such a wimp. Just keep going so we can get him in there.'

They rolled Phil onto his side. Then pushed him into the two-foot-deep hole they had dug on top of the new grave. Jack made sure that his body was in there, but he left enough room for his head to be propped up out of the dirt. Ruby wanted to finish the job and started piling on more.

'Woh, stop putting it over his face or he won't be able to breathe. It will be scary enough for him to wake up in here. You don't actually have to bury the fucker.'

But Ruby carried on. As she poured the dirt over his face, Phil tried to move. He tried to lift his arm, but it was too heavy for him.

'For fuck's sake, Ruby. I'm not joking. Don't put it on his face, OK?'

The more Ruby piled it on, the more Jack brushed it off until he'd had enough.

'That's it—this time I'm really going. You've taken it too far again.' He turned to leave, and Ruby screamed.

'That's typical of you, you're never here when I need you. You always fuck off, just like last time.'

The anger in her eyes was menacing, giving Jack a piercing bout of guilt.

'I'm going to pull the car around, OK. Now leave the fucker there and don't put any on his face. Let him wake up tomorrow surrounded by dead people. That will be bad enough, I promise you.'

When Jack left for the car, Ruby dug behind Phil's head and covered him completely with dirt. She also took the spare dirt off another grave that had been freshly dug and well and truly buried him. Before meeting Jack at the car, she wiped away her prints from the shovel and put it back in the shed. She locked the padlock she had released earlier with the caretaker's key.

'Bye, Phil. Nice knowing you.'

The next morning, Jack drove back to the cemetery. He wanted to check that Phil was OK. Ruby had reassured him that when she left him, he was fine. But he wanted to make sure that he had got out OK. When he reached the grave, a line of cars from a funeral procession was in his way. He could only take a brief glance. There was no sign of Phil. He wasn't sitting up as they had left him, so he assumed he had already left. His conscience was clear, so he carried on driving through.

Chapter Sixteen

The police launched an appeal to find Jack. His photo was released and he was described as a dangerous man, riding a motorbike, wanted in connection with a serious assault that took place in the Carmarthen Bay area. It had been successful, and after a few false leads, a member of the public came forward with some positive information.

There had been a sighting. A lorry driver saw a motorbike parked up with a young man arguing with a girl by the bypass. They had sent officers to the scene, and a police helicopter had scoured the area.

Heather rubbed away at the crick in her neck. The hard plastic chair that she had perched herself on did nothing for her posture. But she wasn't complaining. She had stayed there for most of the night, right next to

Martha. The doctors assured her that although she had been in and out of consciousness; she was going to be OK.

Gareth had informed her of the sighting and asked if she was coming home. Heather had just dismissed his request. She couldn't leave her. And doubted if she could ever leave her again. The attack on Martha had shown Heather how much she cared for her. Maybe it could be different the second time around, she thought. They may stand a chance of a proper relationship now that Martha was not so tied up with the force. But this time Heather was. And she had Gareth to consider too. He had always been there for her. But lately, they had spent more time with other people than together. They had become good friends without the benefits. Heather wanted more. But not from him.

A slight tap on the door had a young PC entering with news.

'Sorry to disturb you, Ma'am, they sent me in to tell you they have found Ruby Lewis. She was down the side of a cliff. They have taken her to intensive care, awaiting surgery.'

'OK, thanks. Was there any sign of the brother?'

'Not that I know of, Ma'am. Do you want me to find out?'

Heather looked over at Martha. 'It's OK, I was leaving now anyway.'

Heather made her way to the intensive care unit. She was pleased that two police officers had been stationed outside her door. As she approached, the door opened and a doctor came out of the room. Heather caught his attention by showing her police badge.

'Can we talk to her yet?'

'No, no, no, under no circumstance. She has suffered a major trauma; a broken arm, broken leg, two fractured ribs, and twenty stitches to her head. She was very lucky that a tree broke her fall, and she landed on soft ground. If she had hit the rocks, she'd be dead.'

After what she had already found out about Ruby, she didn't trust her vulnerability.

'We need to talk to her. Is she at least conscious?'

The doctor looked at his watch. And turned to walk away.

'We've sedated her. Maybe tomorrow if she's up to it.'

That wasn't the answer she needed to hear. The longer she was keeping her secrets, the further away were her chances of catching Jack.

As Heather made her way back to Martha, she saw Karen Lewis being escorted by a female PC into the relative's room. Gareth wasn't far behind.

'Heather, I was just coming to look for you. They have found Bill Ramsgate hanging in his cell. The chief wants you to get over there.'

This was all she needed, she thought.

'Christ, it's never-ending. Tell him it's on my list.'

She looked over to Karen.

'What does she know about her wayward children?'

'All she knows is that Jack is wanted for the assault of a police officer and Ruby was found down the side of a cliff. I didn't mention anything about Ruby being the last person to see Phil as I thought you may want to question her first.'

Heather agreed that was a good call. She didn't want Karen mentioning anything to Ruby if she managed to speak to her before she was questioned.

'Also the landlord from the Royal Oak has phoned in again. He said that Jack was also at the pub that night.

He saw our appeal in the search for Jack and recognised him. This also matches with the CCTV image of the dark car passing through the cemetery. The experts managed to enhance the image and it looked like it was Jack driving the car. Well, I'd better go. I want to be there if he tries to contact his mother. Will I be expecting you home tonight?

Heather shrugged her shoulders. She needed to run home quickly to grab a shower and change her clothes before heading for the prison. All she could give Gareth was a maybe.

She left him to Karen and went back to check on Martha before leaving.

As she popped her head around the door, Martha's eyes opened. Thank God, she thought.

'Hey, you.'

She bent down to kiss her, and Martha welcomed the attention. She couldn't remember much about the attack but knew that Heather had been with her all night.

'Sorry Heather, I shouldn't have got myself involved. It was that Ruby, she's fooled us all.'

Martha explained about their meeting at the college. And that the book had thrown her original investigation in a different direction. Heather assured her she would help her in any way that she could. She knew she had acted in the best interest of the child.

'Don't worry about this now. Get some rest and I'll be back to see you later.'

Martha was thankful that Heather had her back. It would be hard enough trying to get over this injury without adding stress from the past to the mix. She had felt Heather stroking her hair in the night. It had felt comforting and made her realise what she had been missing. If only she had been willing to commit, they may have had a future together, she thought.

* * *

The prison guard that Heather had met on her visit with Ramsgate, buzzed her into the governor's office. She couldn't resist asking him his opinion before he let her through.

'So, do we know if he did this to himself? Or was anyone else involved?'

He stared back at her and ignored the question. He was a strong-looking man with heavy, hooded eyelids. She couldn't tell whether he was keeping something from her or just not a big talker. When the governor walked through the door, he greeted her with a handshake and the guard stepped outside.

'Sorry DI Williams, there were a few things I needed checking out before speaking to you. It seems we've lost the feed to the CCTV cameras just before they found Bill Ramsgates body.'

Heather raised her eyebrows, and the governor continued.

'Without this, we can only assume who was actually on the wing at the time of his death. We had a lot of new inmates coming in the day before. So I'm not sure if there would have been many officers on patrol there. We are quite short-staffed, as you can imagine, with all the government cutbacks.'

As he waffled on, she stopped him in his tracks and asked to see the files of the new arrivals.

As she flicked through them, she came across the transfer file for Wayne Thompson.

'Why was this prisoner put on the same ward as Bill Ramsgate? You do realise that this is the son of the man Ramsgate grassed-up?'

The governor shook his head. 'There must have been some mix up on arrival. This prisoner was supposed to be sent to B Block, on the other side of the prison.'

She rolled her eyes in annoyance.

'Well, evidently not. They allocated him the next cell.'

The governor shuffled his papers around and scratched his head. It was apparent he did not know how this had happened. She had lost all trust in the man to carry out an inside investigation, so needed to start one of her own.

'I will need to speak to Thompson. Can you arrange a place for me to interview him?'

She pointed to the warden outside the door.

'And send someone else to watch the door, will you? I'm not too sure your man out there has good enough manners to facilitate.'

As they led Wayne Thompson into the interview room, he immediately recognised Heather from growing up on the estate.

'Heather, long time no see. How you doing?'

The boy had grown up as sleazy as his father. He looked her up and down and grabbed at his crotch before taking a seat. He leaned over the table to her and whispered away from the guard.

'Are you still pretending to be a virgin? Dexter told us how easy you were when we were beating his head to a pulp. Ah, memories of the estate. I loved that place. And it was you all along shagging that Jamie Taylor. Fuck me, how did you pass to be a copper with your background?'

He was as disgusting as ever. Filling the room with stale sweat and tobacco.

'Nice to see that you haven't changed at all, Thompson. Still, the little scrote running around doing Daddy's dirty business, I see. Where were you when Bill Ramsgate was hanging in his cell, then?'

He folded his arms and sat back in his chair.

'Don't know what you're talking about, Love. Ask the guard. I was with him the whole time. He'll vouch for me—go on.'

Heather knew there was something shifty about that guard. But with no evidence, she also knew she wouldn't be able to prove anything.

'Where's your dad Wayne? Doesn't he realise he can't hide from us forever? We will catch up with him. He hasn't got the sense to move towns, let alone another country, so I know he's around here somewhere.'

'Haven't seen him in years, Love.'

'God, you're still a terrible liar, Thompson. You can tell him from me that when we catch him, he'll be inside for a very long time.'

'Liar am I. Well, that makes two of us, then. Shall I refresh your memory? I wasn't at the building site when Ricky died. I didn't see a thing, officer.'

Heather shifted in her seat as the man recalled Ricky's death.

'That was a long time ago Wayne and you have no right to talk to me like that.'

'But you lied, DI Heather. Now that can't look good on your record.'

'I don't have a clue what you're banging on about, Thompson. I'll be in touch.'

As Heather left the prison, the thoughts of Ricky's demise came to the front of her mind. She could still see the young boy's face as he lay at the bottom of the pit. Even though she had seen many dead bodies since as a police officer, this had always stayed with her.

When she reached her car, she put her hand into her bag to find her keys. Just as she unlocked it, Vic and Steve grabbed her from behind. They aggressively tried to cable tie her wrists together, forcing her onto the bonnet. She kicked and head-butted, but the two men were too strong to get out of their grip.

'Don't make it hard for yourself Heather, Frankie just wants a little chat with you, that is all. Steve pushed her into the back seat while Vic drove the car to the underpass. They had their Lexus waiting for them, and they bundled her into the boot.'

'Right, fancy some chips Steve before we take her in? I'm fucking Hank Marvin.'

Steve gave Vic a judgmental glance. 'That's all you ever think about is eating.'

As they pulled into the back of the haulage yard, they saw Frankie handing money over to Charlie Lane. He took it, then ran off to his car. Frankie had paid him to turn a blind eye and had been using his office as a place to hide out. Ramsgate had hidden a secret compartment under the floor. It held a stash of cash and passports for them all if things had ever gone wrong. Before he had turned informant, he told Frankie where it was and they were supposed to escape the country together.

'Hey boys, do you have our cargo with you?'

Vic banged on the boot before answering. 'She's in the boot, boss.'

'Well, open it up then. Don't keep the girl waiting.'

They released the boot and Heather let out an almighty scream, hoping to get the attention of anyone passing by. She kicked away at her captors and levered herself out of the boot.

Vic grabbed her. So she kicked him hard in the bollocks. Steve threw his arms around her from behind. Holding her in tight restraint. Frankie was sitting on the edge of an open lorry. Steve pushed her towards him, causing her to fall to the ground.

'Heather, long time no see. My, you've grown up to be a beauty. I remember that time I saw in the nick when my boys beat up that ponce Dexter for you.'

Heather spat out the gravel that she had half-swallowed when she hit the floor.

'Don't worry, Love. I'm not gonna hurt you. I just want you to do me a little favour like, seeing as we are old family friends.'

He smiled at her, and she looked at him in disgust. The smile dropped from his face.

'How is your dad these days? He did well with the money I paid him for his accountant services back in the 90s.'

Heather doubted his every word.

'You lying bastard, Frankie. My father would never have had dealings with you.'

'Is that so? You had better ask him yourself then. Did you ever wonder how I spent all that time in the nick? And still came out with a hefty investment waiting for me, then?'

He lit up a cigar and bent down towards the girl, blowing the smoke in her face.

'They bought a new house, didn't they, over in Cardiff? Where do you think he got the money from to pay for that then?'

This confused Heather. Yes, she remembered them suddenly moving up in the world, but to have any dealings with that scumbag just wasn't his style.

'Now listen up, Lovely. All I need you to do is to help me get my boy out of prison. We only transferred him in there to see off that snitch Ramsgate.'

He laughed, knowing what had happened to the thieving grass.

'I want him out of there or Daddy may be facing charges of his own. You get what I'm saying.'

Chapter Seventeen

Ruby sat up in bed while still holding her mother's hand.

'Are you sure you can't remember who did this to you?'

Her mother just wanted to be sure that it wasn't Jack. She had heard all of this terrible news about the crimes that he had committed. And didn't want to think that he could be capable of hurting his sister. Karen had sent Ben to stay with his grandparents. The boy didn't need any more upset. She had hated waking up in an empty house. She wanted her family back where they belong.

'Mam, can you text Phil and ask him to bring in my phone and charger please?'

The mention of his name took Karen by surprise. Surely Ruby would remember such a significant event, she thought.

'Hang on, Love, I just want a word with the doctor.'

The nurse showed Karen into a side room and the doctor who had been monitoring Ruby entered.

'It's very common in cases of trauma like this that a patient would suffer from memory loss. What's the last thing she can remember? Have you asked her?'

Karen put her hand to her mouth. She would hate having to tell Ruby about all the bad things that had happened to them this year.

'Well, she doesn't know that my husband died last month. So that's a start.'

The doctor looked at Karen and took off his glasses.

'Your family has been through a lot lately then, Mrs Jenkins. Maybe this is Ruby's brain, saving her from the trauma whilst mending her body. I'm sure it will only be temporary. She will remember soon.'

The doctor made a point of stating that Ruby should, under no circumstance, be questioned by the police. Her condition was too fragile. They should wait until she could answer the questions put to her with a clear head.

Frankie had received the go-ahead from Heather. He had made the arrangements for their safe transportation out of the country and just needed Heather to stick to her side of the bargain.

'If all this goes to plan, me and the boy will be on that plane this evening. So I don't want either of you to fuck this up. I need that boy to watch my back when we get to wherever the fuck we are going to.'

Vic and Steve stood up for attention. They knew what he had asked of them and were hoping for a cheeky bonus when Frankie leaves.

'We'll make sure it all goes smoothly, Frankie. What time do you want us at the hospital?'

'It's all being arranged, lads. She said she will make sure that the guards turn a blind eye as soon as he's checked in. So one of you needs to nick a wheelchair and a porter's uniform and be on standby. The other one needs to be parked out the back by the loading bay. I'll tell you an exact time later. Then you just have to wait for her signal.'

Steve nodded. But Vic wasn't so sure.

'What if there's no signal? Do we go in and get him? I don't trust that copper. She's a bit of a wild one.'

Frankie reassured them. He had her right where he wanted her.

'Not this time, boys. If she wants her father sleeping peacefully in his bed tonight, she'll co-operate.'

He brought out a hand-drawn map and Vic and Steve took pictures of it on their mobiles.

'Now you know the route to the airfield, don't you? I'll be waiting for you there, OK?'

'Yes, boss, of course.'

Frankie had arranged for Wayne's wrists and ankles to be smashed in by an old mate at the prison. He didn't tell his son beforehand as he couldn't trust him opening his big mouth. There was no way they would put cuffs on him in that state. He just needed to put up with the pain down to the hospital, then Frankie's boys would break him out.

Heather had been visiting Martha; keeping her up to date on the murder of Phil Jenkins. They heard about Ruby's amnesia and hoped that it had included the visit regarding the book. This way, they would catch her for the second murder. But sadly, forget the mistake made in the past.

The door opened, and PC Reid entered with a message.

'Wayne Thompson has arrived in A & E Ma'am. You asked to be told when he arrives.'

'Thank you, Matt. Can you get a message to Gareth and tell him too, please? I'll give you his number.'

He told her he already had it. And Heather felt a sense of guilt in his voice. She wouldn't mind if Gareth had been seeing the man. That was his business. Who was she to comment after she had come to terms with her true feelings for Martha? she thought. It would be cruel to keep Gareth waiting. She would have to decide whether to set him free to love whoever he wanted to. She was sure that Gareth had felt it too. Times were changing. New laws were being put into place about homosexuality in the workplace. There was no longer a need to hide as much as when they first joined the force.

Heather made her way down to the accident and emergency department. Wayne Thompson had a prison guard on either side of him, while waiting to be examined by the triage nurse.

She led him to a cubicle and pulled back the blue mottled curtain.

'You're going to have to let go of him gentlemen or I won't be able to examine him properly. Just wait outside. He'll be OK.'

They gave the man his privacy and Heather flashed her police badge and spoke to the guards.

'Is that Wayne Thompson in there?'

'Yes, we've just been chucked out by the nurse.'

She pointed at the coffee machine just outside the ward.

'I'll keep watch from here, lads. You two get us a coffee.'

As soon as they left through the double doors, Heather went behind the curtain and asked the nurse to step outside for a chat.

'What do you think about his injuries, nurse? Do you think he will have to stay in?'

'No, they are mainly superficial by the look of it. I won't know for definite until the porter takes him to x-ray.'

She didn't really care about the answer, as she was texting Steve to let him know Wayne was unaccompanied. Their plan was working, and the breakout was about to happen.

As the porter helped Wayne into the chair, Heather could clearly see that it was Vic in the uniform. She turned a blind eye as he rushed him through the corridor under the noses of the prison guards. They were still standing at the machine, getting their coffee.

When they returned, the nurse informed them he was having an x-ray. And that they would not be allowed to enter the room. They were to wait a few minutes outside of the door. During that time, Vic would have had him back in the car and on his way to Frankie.

Gareth was waiting for Heather in the car park and had a close view of Wayne Thompson in his getaway car.

As Heather approached, he started the engine.

'Quick, get in. We can tail them as soon as they get to the gates. Just keep your head down.'

Heather put on Gareth's old cap and pushed her hair underneath.

At the field, Gareth waited until they met up with Frankie. He signalled to the other cars that were lying in wait to be ready to make the ambush.

As soon as they pulled in, four police cars came from around the corner and blocked them in.

Heather shouted over to Frankie to get out of the car and lie on the floor with his hands behind his head.

They had already apprehended Wayne and locked him in the back of the police car with Vic and Steve. Hand and ankle cuffs firmly attached.

Frankie stood out of the car with his hands on his head.

'You're making a huge mistake, Heather. Daddy won't be happy with you.'

Gareth, who was standing next to Heather, nudged her. 'What's that about?'

'Absolutely nothing Gareth.'

After her proposal, at the haulage yard, she spoke to her dad. He said that he had done Frankie a small favour in the 90s. But nothing illegal. He had helped him bury a petty crime that would be laughed out of court today, so he wasn't worried in the slightest.

Frankie's intimidation had fallen on deaf ears. With her dad's reputation safe, she went straight to the chief to hatch a plan. They would bait and catch Frankie by using his own son's fake escape. Only trusted individuals knew about it. They kept the prison guards in the dark. It was the only way to ensure its safe execution.

As they assisted Frankie out of the car, a motorbike swerved to the side of them. The rider took a shot at Frankie and he fell to his knees. The second shot killed him outright. He dropped the gun, removed his helmet, and put his hands in the air. It was Jack.

He now had a police marksman pointing straight at him, waiting for his next move.

'The fucker deserved it!' he shouted. 'He was a paedophile and his actions wrecked mine and my sister's life. She's dead because of him. She wasn't to blame for anything. I want it on record that it was me who killed my fathers, Craig and Phil.'

He dropped to his knees and held his head in his hands. As Heather approached him, he quickly grabbed the gun from in front of him and shot himself in the head.

Brain matter landed at her feet. With all the commotion, she didn't get the chance to tell him that Ruby was still alive. If she had, maybe things wouldn't have gotten that far.

They released Ruby from the hospital, into the arms of her mother. Karen knew nothing of the crimes they nearly accused her of and grieved hard for her son. The amnesia continued and although some days Karen had thought that Ruby was back; she insisted she had still lost her memory of the past.

Because of the confession from Jack and the evidence they had of his whereabouts, they were no longer looking for any other suspects. They recognised him as the killer of Phil Jenkins and Craig Lewis.

The goods bought with the money that Phil helped launder were seized by the police as illegal gain. Karen, and what was left of her family, were put into emergency housing on the Beechwood estate. They were back where it all began and devastated by the decline.

Martha was released from the hospital with one less of her remaining seven lives gone. Living to fight another day.

Heather tried hard to make it work with Gareth, but all she could think of was Martha. He had been spending a lot of time with PC Matt Reid. So they both agreed to separate. They would live a life that was more true to themselves.

Martha finally told Heather that she had been the only one she had regretted letting go. And after finding out that her goat's name was actually Gareth, she believed her.

The Beechwood estate had lost its main man; leaving behind a pair of boots for the next wannabe gangster to fill. There was always that threat. Ruby knew this more than anyone. And after her old friend Chloe came back for her father's funeral, things were about to get heavy on the estate. Frankie was gone. But Chloe had her father's money to spend, and a debt to settle with Ruby. She wasn't the gullible little girl anymore and had lived her life closer to the edge than many.

Beechwood Estate Series

Book 1

Jamie's Story

Book 2

The Past Should Stay Dead

Book 3

Back From The Edge

(Coming Soon)

Thank you for your support.

If you enjoyed this novel, please leave a review on Amazon and/or Goodreads. I read every review and it will help new readers discover my book.

Take Care

Kim x

Printed in Great Britain
by Amazon

78250959R00171